MAY - - 2022

Goddess Girls

ARTEMIS
THE LOYAL

Goddess Girls

ARTEMIS
THE LOYAL

JOAN HOLUB & SUZANNE WILLIAMS

Aladdin

NEW YORK   LONDON   TORONTO   SYDNEY   NEW DELHI

ALADDIN

An imprint of Simon & Schuster Children's Publishing Division

1230 Avenue of the Americas, New York, NY 10020

First Aladdin hardcover edition December 2013

Text copyright © 2011 by Joan Holub and Suzanne Williams

Cover illustration copyright © 2011 by Glen Hanson

Also available in an Aladdin paperback edition.

For information about special discounts for bulk purchases, please contact Simon & Schuster Special Sales at 1-866-506-1949 or business@simonandschuster.com.

The Simon & Schuster Speakers Bureau can bring authors to your live event. For more information or to book an event contact the Simon & Schuster Speakers Bureau at 1-866-248-3049 or visit our website at www.simonspeakers.com.

Designed by Karin Paprocki

The text of this book was set in Baskerville Handcut Regular.

Manufactured in the United States of America 0715 FFG

2 4 6 8 10 9 7 5 3

Library of Congress Control Number 2011935558

ISBN 978-1-4424-8594-5 (hc)

ISBN 978-1-4424-3377-9 (pbk)

ISBN 978-1-4424-3378-6 (eBook)

To Gabriela Sagun and Cecelia Sagun

–J. H. and S. W.

CONTENTS

1

No Girls Allowed

"RACE YOU TO THE SPORTS FIELDS!" ARTEMIS challenged her twin brother, Apollo, as they crossed Mount Olympus Academy's courtyard on Wednesday afternoon. Practices for the Olympic Games, which would take place on Saturday, were now in progress. Talented athletes from all over Greece, Mount

Olympus, and other magical realms, had come to MOA to compete.

Apollo crouched in a runner's stance with his fingertips touching the courtyard's marble tiles. "You're on."

Artemis crouched too. "Ready. Set. *Go!*" she shouted.

They took off at the exact same moment. Both immortal twins flew across the courtyard and down a crowded grassy hill, legs pumping. Artemis's three dogs kept pace beside them. They liked to run too!

The twins' best sport was archery, but Artemis loved any kind of athletic competition. As archers, she and her brother were evenly matched. However, with some extra effort she could usually beat him in a race. Right now he was a couple of feet behind her. Slowly, she began to widen her lead, her eyes on the sports fields.

Ahead of them, colorful banners waved high on the flagpoles that lined the edges of the largest field. Each had a logo for a particular sport. However, there was no logo for archery. It wasn't an Olympic event. Not that it mattered in Artemis's case. She had no chance at winning in the Olympics. Why? Because all those competitors here for the Games? Every single one of them was a boy. Not a girl among them. Girls were not allowed to compete in the Games.

Thinking about it, Artemis's shoulders tightened. It wasn't fair!

She glanced back at Apollo. *Ye gods!* He was gaining on her! Just then Ares, who was the fastest runner at MOA, saw them coming. A crowd of students had gathered alongside one of the tracks to watch the foot race practices and he was among them. Grinning at

Apollo, he cupped his hands around his mouth and called out: "Go! You can beat her. She's a *girl*!"

That did it! Gritting her teeth, Artemis gathered all her determination. Her eyes locked on the finish line. With a huge burst of speed, she sprinted across the edge of the field, well ahead of Apollo.

"Whoa!" shouted Ares. He jumped back to avoid her plowing into him before she could skid to a stop.

As she stood catching her breath, Artemis shot him a superior glance. "I may only be a *girl*, but I won, didn't I?"

"Uh-huh, sure. Good race," Ares said lamely.

Artemis had noticed that whenever a girl was good at sports, boys seemed to lose interest. Turning, she saw Apollo standing behind her. His face was as red as her favorite chiton.

"Thanks a lot!" he grumbled. "Way to embarrass me in front of my friends!"

What? she thought. *I'm supposed to lose, just so he can save face? No way!*

"Hey, Artemis, over here!" Athena called from the stands. A light breeze blew a lock of the goddessgirl's naturally wavy brown hair across her cheek, and she pushed it back with one hand as she waved with her other. Still annoyed at her brother, Artemis stomped off to sit with her friend. All the event practices were going on at the same time, and Athena was watching the discus-throwing. She scooted over to make room for Artemis.

A godboy named Atlas was up first. He held a discus—a disk about the size of a dinner plate—in his right hand. As the girls watched, he sprang into action. Twisting his body, he turned in a full circle to gather momentum. "Argh!" he grunted. Then with a mighty heave, he flung the discus high and long. It flew half the length of the field!

The other MOA boys had come over to cheer his attempt. "Way to go, Atlas!" Apollo called out. He punched his fist in the air.

"That rocked!" called Ares.

Artemis glared at them. Sure, they got all excited when a *boy* did well at sports! *Hmph!*

Suddenly, Ares seemed to forget all about the discus and his head jerked in Artemis's direction. She straightened. *What's he looking at me for?* But then she realized he was staring at something beyond her. Looking over her shoulder, she saw her friend Aphrodite approaching. Half the boys on the field stopped what they were doing to watch the goddessgirl stroll toward Athena and Artemis. Her long hair shone like gold in the sunlight, the hem of her bright blue chiton fluttered with her every step, and her sparkling blue eyes smiled at Ares as she gave him a little wave of her blue-nail-polished fingers.

Those boys probably thought all girls should be girly-girls like Aphrodite and leave athletics to the guys. "It's not fair," Artemis complained aloud.

"I know," said Athena, grinning. "She does get attention. But Aphrodite was just born gorgeous. She can't help it that she's the prettiest girl at MOA."

"No, not that," said Artemis. "I meant it's not fair that only boys get to compete in the Olympics. I'm a good athlete. So are other girls around here. Why shouldn't we be able to participate in the Games?"

"Maybe the boys are afraid you'd win," said Aphrodite, smiling as she joined them.

7

"Maybe we *would* win," Artemis said earnestly.

"You're serious?" said Aphrodite, staring at her in surprise. "You'd really like to be in the Games?"

"You bet your sweet lip gloss I would," said Artemis. At first her dogs had been content to lay at her feet, but now they began to paw at her, bored. Flipping her shiny black hair out of her eyes, she pulled a bone-shaped ball from her pocket and tossed it to the grassy area outside the sports fields. The magical ball zigzagged, bouncing high and then low. Her three dogs went crazy and tore after it.

Athena shook her head. "No chance. Zeus decided long ago that the Olympics are just for boys. Always have been, always will be." She gestured toward the long, giant billboard at the far side of the field. It depicted glorious scenes from past Olympic Games throughout history. Boys wrestling. Boys running track. Boys throwing javelins. Boys, boys, boys!

Athena was probably right, though. Zeus was her dad, after all, so she'd know. And not only was he the principal of MOA, he was also Kings of the Gods and Ruler of the Heavens. Basically, his word was law.

"But doesn't it make you mad?" asked Artemis, feeling her irritation rise. "Even a little?"

Aphrodite shrugged. "Not really. I don't want to compete. I'd rather watch all the boys sweating it out from a comfy seat in the stands."

"I never thought about it before," Athena said, combing her fingers through her hair. "But Artemis does have a point. If we did want to compete, we should be— Oh, no!" Catching sight of her crush, Heracles, farther down the field, she gasped. A scaly dragon-boy had just snatched him up in his sharp talons! Muscles bulging, Heracles quickly reversed things, flipping the dragon-boy over his head and slamming him to the ground.

Flames shot from the dragon-boy's snout, singeing the ends of Heracles' hair.

Athena bounced excitedly in her seat and yelled, "Yes! Pin him!"

Glancing over his shoulder at her, Heracles grinned and gave her a thumbs-up.

Just then, with ears flapping and tails wagging, Artemis's dogs returned. Her beagle, Amby, was in the lead with the ball, which he dropped in the palm of her hand. "Good job," she said, unfazed by the dog slobber that now covered the ball.

Aphrodite scooted away a little, but didn't say anything. Everyone knew she had an aversion to dogs. And dog slobber.

"Thirsty, boys?" Artemis asked, noticing how hard her pooches were panting. Hopping up, she led them to an oval-shaped stone fountain a few feet away. It had been designed in the shape of a big *O* (for Olympics) by Poseidon, godboy of the sea, especially for these Games. At its center, water sprayed outward in loops and twists from its many spigots, seeming to dance in the air for a few seconds before tumbling back into the pool below.

Poseidon had waded into the fountain's waters and was tinkering with the pump mechanism, trying to make each spigot sound a different musical note when water spurted from it. All around him, magical fish were practicing tricks, which they would perform during the Games. And every now and then a weird sound or sour note honked from the pipes as he worked.

Pocketing the ball, Artemis reached into the pool at the base of the fountain to scoop up some water. "Here," she said, holding her cupped hands out so each dog in turn could drink from them. When they'd finished lapping up the water, she pulled the ball out again. Winding up, she pitched it downfield. Amby scampered after it, but Nectar, Artemis's greyhound, beat him and her bloodhound, Suez, to it. Just as Nectar was about to snatch it, the teasing ball spun away, moving up into the stands.

"Hey, you've got a pretty good arm for a girl," a mortal boy named Actaeon called out. He and a god-boy named Hades had apparently been watching her from where they stood by the sand pit, waiting their turns at the long jump. At any other time, Artemis might have taken Actaeon's words as a compliment. But at these boy-only games, and given what Ares had said after her race with Apollo—it made her steaming mad.

"What's that supposed to mean?" she shouted back. "You don't think girls can throw?"

But Actaeon didn't hear because right then a cheer rose up from the crowd in the stands over at the track.

Another practice footrace had begun and Ares, as usual, had broken out in front of the pack of runners.

"Go, go, *go!*" Aphrodite yelled from the stands. She and Ares had an on-again, off-again relationship that had been more on than off lately—ever since Ares had sung a sweet song about her at the last school dance. "That's the way!" she cheered. Because of course that's all girls could do at the Games. Cheer for the boys.

Grr, thought Artemis.

"Has Hades jumped yet?" someone asked. Artemis looked over her shoulder to see Persephone. She was standing nearby, shielding her green eyes with her pale hand as she looked toward the sand pit. A gold necklace with a GG charm encircled her throat and glinted in the sunlight. "I couldn't get here any earlier. I stayed late after Garden-ology class in fourth period to help Ms. Thallo unpack a new shipment of seeds."

"No worries," said Athena, joining them just then from the stands. "He hasn't had his turn yet." The three girls and Aphrodite were best buds as well as the most popular goddessgirls at MOA, and they all wore the look-alike GG necklaces.

"Oh, good." Persephone's red curls bounced as she went up on tiptoe, waving to catch Hades' eye. He sent her a nod in return, looking a little relieved. "I didn't want to miss it," she told the girls. "He thinks I'm his good-luck charm."

Artemis sighed as Nectar trotted up with the ball and dropped it at her feet. Weren't any of her friends as bothered as she was that they could only support the boys' efforts rather than participate in the Games themselves? As she bent to grab the ball, the ground suddenly shifted under her feet, knocking her off balance.

Stomp! Stomp! Stomp!

"Godzooks!" she exclaimed. Forgetting all about the unfairness of the boys-only games, she threw her arms wide to keep from falling. Beside her, water whooshed up in a wave and splashed from the fountain's pool to slap the ground.

Looking around, she found the source of the rumbling. Giants! *Two* of them. Each was twice as tall as the tallest godboy at MOA, with shoulders twice as wide, too. And they were coming this way.

What can they possibly want?

2

The Giants

PERSEPHONE'S EYES WIDENED. "GIANTS?"

"They're so huge, they've got to be!" said Artemis.
The only giant she'd ever seen outside of a picture in a
textscroll was their Hero-ology teacher, Mr. Cyclops.
But he was shorter than these giants and had only
one eye—one *humongous* eye—in the middle of his forehead. These giants had the usual two. Plus, they both

had curly, bright red hair and grumpy expressions. Mr. Cyclops was bald. And he was usually only grumpy if you didn't turn in your homework.

The other goddessgirls seemed just as wary of them as Artemis was, and no wonder. Giants had a bad reputation.

Boom! Boom! As the two giants stomped onto the field, the ground trembled with every step they took. The sound echoed across the now-quiet sports fields. No one moved. The practice games had come to a complete standstill, all eyes riveted on the enormous newcomers. The giants finally halted by the fountain—mere feet away from where Artemis, Persephone, and Athena were standing!

"We're here for the wrestling," one of them announced. In spite of his big, burly size, his voice was high and girlish. Artemis heard some of the boys on the field giggle in nervous surprise. Otherwise, the giant's words were met with silence.

Ares glared at the giants, his arms folded across his chest. Hades and Apollo eyed them with suspicion. There was a long history of mistrust between gods and giants. In Hero-ology class, they'd learned this dated back to a time in the distant past when the Olympian gods overthrew a group of rulers called the Titans. Because Mr. Cyclops's family had taken the Olympians' side in the war, Zeus allowed him to teach at MOA. But the rest of the giants had fought on the Titan side. And though Zeus and the Olympian gods had won the war, they had never quite forgiven the giants. And vice versa.

"How dare they show up here!" Artemis heard some-one mutter.

"We've come to officially enter the competition, just like everyone else," said the giant who'd been silent till now. This one had a voice almost as deep as Zeus's, but neither he nor his companion could've been more than twelve to fourteen years old, tops.

When no one else spoke up, Artemis began to wonder if they were going to stand around like this all day. As far as she knew, there were no actual rules against giants entering the Games, so there was only one thing to do. She pointed toward Heracles and the other wrestlers. "Wrestling's over there," she told the giants.

"Much obliged, miss," said the deep-voiced giant.

Artemis grinned.

"What's so funny?" he asked, as if he suspected she might be laughing at him.

"Nothing," she told him. "It's just that no one my age has ever called me *miss* before."

"Oh." He grinned back then, flashing white teeth. "It's proper etiquette where I come from. I'm Otus.

And this is my brother, Ephialtes. And you are?"

"Artemis." Out of the corner of her eye, she glimpsed Apollo giving her a *what-are-you-doing-talking-to-giants* look. Like him, she'd been primed to mistrust giants. She'd imagined them to be ugly and ill-mannered, but Otus seemed very polite. And both giants were actually pretty cute—not that she cared!—with puppy-dog brown eyes, strong jaws, and lots of muscles.

They looked so much alike they had to be twins, she realized. Just like Apollo and her. Only while these giants were identical, she and Apollo were not. The only traits *they* had in common were glossy black hair, dark eyes, and archery skills.

Ephialtes sent the goddessgirls a snooty glance. "I thought these Games were guys-only," he said, one big hand scratching his ribs. Then his high voice turned snarky. "Although godboys *do* play like girls now that I think about it." He laughed at his own lame joke.

"Huh?" said Artemis, putting both hands on her hips and scrunching her face into a frown. The athletes on the field grumbled and began to move closer to the giants, as if they expected trouble. Or were thinking of starting some. She felt someone beside her and saw that Aphrodite had come over.

"Maybe somebody better get my dad," murmured Athena, sounding worried. Artemis glanced around, looking for Zeus or a teacher, but then she remembered there was a staff meeting that afternoon.

"These Games. Guys-only," Ephialtes repeated with insulting slowness, as if he thought MOA gods and god-desses were not very bright. "In fact, why are you girls even out here? Shoo!" He flicked his fingers toward the goddessgirls as if to sweep them off the field.

The girls and most of the boys, too, stared at him,

dumbfounded by his rudeness. Since Otus didn't contradict Ephialtes, Artemis figured he must feel the same way. So much for good manners!

"We're just here to watch," Persephone replied, trying to calm things.

"Yeah. It's the only thing we *can* do, since girls aren't allowed to compete in the Games!" Artemis couldn't help adding.

"Way it should be," Ephialtes said haughtily.

Artemis saw Ares nudge Apollo and roll his eyes. Was he annoyed at the giant for talking to her that way? Or did he think *she* was being annoying for implying that girls should be able to compete in the Games? Well, these boys and giants were *all* annoying buttheads if they thought she was just going to stand here and take whatever they dished out.

Her fist tightened around the ball she still held in

her hand. Without thinking twice, she wound up and threw the ball with all her might. It zoomed toward the giants, right over Ephialtes' head, parting his hair and making him duck in surprise. And still the ball flew on, out over the sports fields. Long seconds later, it finally landed an awesome full length of the field away! Thinking that another game had begun, her three pooches chased after it.

"Were you aiming that at me?" shrieked Ephialtes, taking a step toward her. Artemis just shrugged.

Aphrodite, Persephone, and Athena sidled closer as if fearing trouble. At the same time, Ares, Hades, Apollo, and Actaeon moved to flank the girls protectively.

"No. Wait," said Artemis, suddenly worried. Maybe she should try to smooth things over before a real fight broke out.

Otus, the deep-voiced giant, took his brother's arm.

"Don't be a twit, bro," he said. "She's just a girl. Girls can't even aim, much less send a ball that far on purpose. It was just a lucky throw."

That did it! Artemis immediately lost interest in smoothing anything.

She took a giant step toward the girly-voiced giant. "Yeah, you're *lucky* I didn't aim for your nose!" she yelled. "For your information, that ball went right where I meant it to. And there are plenty of girls at MOA who can throw as well. We'd probably beat half the boys in the Games if we were allowed to compete in them."

Ephialtes burst into laughter. He elbowed his brother. "Did you hear that, Otus? She thinks girls should be in the Games!" Between giggles, he managed to tell her, "There's no way that's gonna happen, girly. Besides, aren't you worried you might mess up your hair?"

"Shut it, giant!" shouted Ares. He pushed his way to

the front of the crowd till he was standing nose-to-belt-buckle with the giant. "You can't talk to her that way! Zeus commanded that the Games be boys-only. As is right. But you're only guests here. Only giants. *We're* the gods and we rule, so don't try to boss us around! Not even the girls!"

Ephialtes' eyes flashed. "Oh, yeah?"

"Yeah!" said Ares, scowling.

"Uh-oh," Artemis heard Aphrodite say. "I know that look on Ares' face. When he gets mad, it's *war.*"

In a show of solidarity, a dozen other MOA boys—Apollo, Hades, Actaeon, and Poseidon among them—stepped up beside Ares. Probably most of the boys at the Academy agreed with the boys-only Olympics rule. But if anyone was going to make fun of Artemis's idea, the boys wanted it to be them, not these outsiders.

"You leave my sister alone," Apollo said, daring to

give the giant's belly a hard jab with the tip of his finger.

Artemis would have appreciated him coming to her defense more if she'd thought that he saw her side of things. But she had a feeling he didn't.

"Stop this!" Persephone called, as things heated up even more.

The boys and the giants ignored her as they circled around each other, eyes glaring and fists tightening. Artemis didn't see who threw the first punch, but as soon as it happened a huge fight broke out.

The giants were fierce brawlers. Standing back-to-back, they landed blows, knocking several boys over like toothpicks. Ares placed a kick to Otus's shin. As the giant roared in pain and hopped on one foot, Apollo aimed a kick at his other shin. But before he could connect, Ephialtes snatched Apollo up by the back of his tunic so that his feet dangled off the ground.

"You leave my brother alone!" Artemis shouted in alarm. Summoning up the bravery she was famed for, she doubled up her fists, then took a step toward the giant.

Ephialtes grinned down at her. "You gonna do his fighting for him?"

Artemis stuck out her chin. "If I *have* to!" She automatically reached over her shoulder for a magic arrow, then remembered she'd left her quiver and bow back in the dorm because she'd been in a hurry to get here. It was one of the rare times she'd gone off without them.

The giant snorted. "Sorry—I don't fight girls. Or boys who let girls do their fighting for them." He lowered Apollo until he was about a foot off the ground, then dropped him so he tumbled to his knees. "Run to your big, strong sister now," he said, patting him on the head, "so she can protect you." He laughed again, and to Artemis's horror, so did some of the godboys. Then both giants sauntered off toward the wrestling area.

Apollo turned red as he leaped to his feet. Ramming both hands into the pockets of his tunic, he shot her a hard look. Then he stalked off in the opposite direction of the giants.

Godzooks! For the second time in less than an hour, it seemed she'd embarrassed him.

"Help, help! Can you protect *me* too, Artemis!" one of the godboys called out.

Two red roses bloomed in her cheeks. "Who said that?" she demanded, confronting the crowd.

"Actaeon did!" another voice yelled. Suddenly,

Actaeon charged out of the crowd and slammed into her. The impact pushed her backward against the edge of the fountain. Her arms spun in the air for a second as Actaeon tried to grab her, but there was no saving her. *Splash!* She landed on her butt in the pool. *Splash! Splash! Splash!* Thinking it was a game, her dogs jumped in too, flinging water everywhere as they romped.

Her embarrassment quickly turning to rage, Artemis struggled to her feet. Her hair was dripping wet, and her chiton clung to her like a big, wet ambrosia noodle. And there was something flopping around on her head—one of the magical fish!

Actaeon stared at her in dismay for a split-second before bursting into laughter. The other godboys joined in, laughing too. Artemis shook her head wildly, until the fish disentangled itself from her hair. Iridescent scales flashing in the sunlight, it backflipped off her head to rejoin its friends.

Still chuckling, Actaeon reached over the side of the fountain to help her out, but she pushed him away. Glaring at him, she said, "You have a weird sense of humor, mortal."

"Sorry, Artemis," he said, looking like he was trying hard now not to smile. "It *was* kind of fishy, um, I mean funny, if you think about it. Let me help." He reached for her again.

"Okay." Pretending to accept his help this time, she grabbed his hand with both of her own. Then she leaned backward and tugged, trying to pull *him* into the pool too. Unfortunately, her wet hands slipped. *Splash!* Back in the fountain. On her butt again. And a second later, a magical fish leaped onto her nose. She stared at it, cross-eyed and thoroughly humiliated. "Get off. I'm not part of your act!"

Using her nose as a diving board, the fish flipped back into the pool. This only made Actaeon, and everyone else, laugh harder. Her eyes darted fire at him as she scrambled to her feet again, and climbed over the side of the fountain.

"Never mind him," Aphrodite said. Rushing forward, she and Athena took Artemis's arms and tugged her away before she could give Actaeon the thrashing he deserved.

"Never mind *any* of them," said Athena, glaring at the crowd and the giants over on the field, who also appeared to be watching.

"Let's just go," Persephone said softly. "You can change clothes back at the dorm."

Too angry to see reason, Artemis pulled away. Her blue-black eyes drilled into Actaeon's gray ones. All of her annoyance at her brother, these boys, and the giants suddenly focused itself on him. Before she could stop herself, she was chanting a magic spell. And reaching a hand toward him.

"Whosoever my hand doth tag.

Turn that boy into a stag."

A look of alarm flitted across Actaeon's face, and he tried to dodge her touch. But Artemis lunged forward and tapped him on the arm. "Tag—you're a stag," she sing-songed.

Instantly, Actaeon dropped to all fours. As his limbs became sleekly furred, his hands and feet changed to hooves. The features of his face lengthened, and an enormous set of antlers sprouted from the top of his head. When the change was complete, Actaeon-the-stag gave a bleat and leaped away. Immediately, Artemis's dogs gave chase, thinking this was some new game. To her surprise, her dogs weren't the only ones to give chase.

"Ephialtes, come back!" yelled Otus, the better-mannered giant. But his brother ignored him. His big feet shook the ground as he dashed from the sports field and thudded off after the stag.

Godsamighty! thought Artemis. *What have I done?*

3

Brother vs. Sister

THOUGH ARTEMIS WAS STILL FURIOUS AT ACTAEON—

and being soaking wet and surrounded by the smell

of wet dog made everything worse—she had to stop

Ephialtes. Everyone knew that giants were notori-

ous hunters. She hated to think what might happen if

Actaeon were caught!

Quickly, she shouted out a new chant:

"Though this won't give me any joy,

Reverse the spell—turn stag to boy!"

Ephialtes was gaining on Actaeon and was just about to grab his antlers when stag began to morph back into boy. The giant halted, a disappointed look on his face as the antlers disappeared and Actaeon regained his true form.

At that very moment Coach Triathlon, who taught Olympics-ology at MOA, burst out of the doors of the gymnasium heading for the field. He was whistling, obviously unaware of all that had gone on. He paused as he passed Artemis, eyeing her soaked condition in surprise. "What happened to you?"

"My dogs got into the fountain," she replied. Technically, it wasn't a lie, and it seemed to satisfy the coach, who moved on to speak to the two giants. Artemis looked toward the spot where Actaeon had been minutes before, but he was gone now.

Fighting was against MOA rules. Since no one wanted to risk cancellation of the Games, not one of the students added a word of explanation. Not even Pheme, the goddessgirl of gossip, piped up. Probably because Persephone had wrapped both hands around the girl's mouth!

After Coach Triathlon handed out lists of teams and individual matchups for workouts the following day, practice was officially over. The athletes and students broke up into groups and started back toward MOA. As the two giants headed off in the opposite direction, everyone else buzzed with excitement about all that had happened.

Except for the squishing sounds her feet made in

her wet sandals, Artemis was silent as she walked. Sensing her mood, her friends didn't try to get her to talk, but she felt their concerned eyes on her. Even her dogs were unusually subdued as they trailed the four goddessgirls.

What had just happened back there? She wished she'd never gone to the field today at all. She needed to find Apollo and make sure he was okay. And she guessed she needed to see if Actaeon was too, even though he sort of deserved what she'd done.

When the girls reached the courtyard, Apollo appeared, his hands still fisted deep in the pockets of his tunic. "Got a minute?" he asked Artemis in a tight voice. His dark eyes, so like hers, were flashing with emotion.

"Right now?" she asked, looking down at her dripping chiton.

He nodded.

Artemis glanced at her friends. "Would you take my dogs up to my room for me?"

"No problem," said Persephone. Since befriending Hades' dog, Cerberus, she'd become quite a dog-lover herself.

As soon as they were alone, Apollo ripped into her. "Think you could do anything more to embarrass me today?" he yelled.

Artemis drew back in surprise. "Huh? If you're still mad about our race, I won that fair and square. And if you're mad about what just happened with the giants, you ought to be thanking me instead. I wasn't just going to stand by and let that giant cream you! What did you expect?"

"Not for my *sister* to come to my rescue, that's for sure! I can take care of myself."

"Uh-huh. I saw. *Everyone* saw." Why should she say she was sorry? She'd *helped* him!

"Why don't you just stay off the field from now on?" he ranted. "Girls don't belong out there anyway."

Ooh! It was the wrong thing to say. She got up in his face. "And why shouldn't girls be in the Olympics? I'm a good athlete and you know it."

"Well, Zeus is the boss and he made the Olympics boys-only. You're not a boy, so stop trying to act like one. And another thing—what you did to Actaeon was inexcusable! You know what I think?"

"I can't wait to hear!" she said sarcastically.

"I think you did it just because he likes you."

"What?" Artemis felt her cheeks flush. She looked around. Students were going to and fro across the courtyard around them. She hoped no one had heard. "No, he doesn't!" she hissed.

Apollo sent her a superior look, like he knew something she didn't. Did boys talk about the girls they liked in the same way girls talked about boys?

"You're crazy!" Artemis said, looking away from him. "I turned him into a stag because he deserved it. He pushed me into the fountain!"

"Well, you're just lucky no one ratted you out to the coach."

Feeling cold drops of water streaming down her legs, Artemis reached down and wrung out the hem of her chiton. "I can't believe you're not backing me up. Actaeon doesn't like me. He was laughing at me!"

"Like you made the other guys laugh at me by coming to my rescue?" Apollo clasped his hands over his heart and began speaking in a high voice meant to mimic her own. "Oh, big, bad giant, please put my poor defenseless brother down or I'll beat you up."

"It wasn't like that and you know it! I was just—"

"Hey!" someone called out to them. They looked over to see Heracles coming their way. Earlier, he'd been wearing the school's wrestling uniform—a stretchy blue and gold tunic—but now he was dressed in his usual manner, wearing a lion-skin cape with jaws that fitted his head like a helmet. *Doesn't he ever get hot in that furry thing?* Artemis wondered.

Though Aphrodite often made fun of Heracles' fashion sense, Apollo and the other boys all thought the cape was cool. They admired Heracles for his many feats of strength and courage. As part of the twelve labors he'd had to complete in order to remain at MOA, he'd recently battled death-dealing birds and a dangerous Cretan bull!

But Artemis didn't really feel like talking to anyone now. She felt hurt. And confused. She and Apollo usually had each other's backs. It felt weird that he wasn't supporting her. Couldn't he see that his anger was way out of proportion to what she'd done?

"Hey, I'm not interrupting, am I?" Heracles asked, glancing from one twin to the other.

"Nope," said Apollo. "What's up?"

"Coach told me you hadn't signed up for an Olympic event yet," he said to Apollo.

What? Artemis glanced at her brother in surprise. Every boy at MOA was expected to compete in at least one event. She'd assumed Apollo would choose the foot races and maybe the long jump. But come to think of it, he'd never told her which events he was going out for.

"The wrestling team could use some new blood," Heracles hinted. "It's not too late to sign on."

Apollo made a wry face. "Thanks, but wrestling's not really my thing."

Heracles grinned. "Can't say I blame you. Those giants are going to be stiff competition this year."

He glanced at Artemis. "Too bad you can't join in the Games to protect us from them, huh?" He laughed, not seeming to notice that his joke fell flat. "And it's too bad for your brother there's no archery event. You'd be his only real competition, but you can't compete!" He smiled at her, like she should be pleased at the compliment. She scowled at him. Why were boys so dense? He obviously didn't realize that his words were hurtful to both her *and* Apollo!

There was an awkward silence as neither twin responded to Heracles. "Well, uh, later, then," Heracles said at last. With a wave, he loped back toward the main building.

Once again, Apollo's face had turned red and splotchy with embarrassment and anger. "Hey," said

Artemis. "I'm sure he didn't mean that the way it sounded."

Apollo scowled at her. "Maybe it's time we did more stuff on our own," he said. "Starting now." Turning his back on her, he stalked off toward a trail at the side of the courtyard. Artemis hurried after him. "But—"

"Stop following me!" Apollo yelled over his shoulder.

"Fine!" she yelled back. "Be that way!" For the moment she was too mad to care if he ever came back! Still, there was a lump in her throat as she whipped around. She crossed the courtyard, then climbed the granite steps to the school's massive bronze front doors. Venting her frustration, she yanked them open.

She entered the main hall to find a bunch of students crowded around a sign that hung on the enormous column by the trophy case, where notices were always posted. Drawing closer, she saw that it was an announcement of a special event that was to be the grand finale of this year's Olympics.

"What's a *Python-o-thon*?" she heard someone ask. Curious herself, she began to read:

Attention Athletes:

There's a new event this year

in the Olympic Games:

THE PYTHON-O-THON!

Think you have what it takes to tangle with

the biggest, baddest, trickiest serpent ever–

The Parnassus Python?

Then enter this contest if you dare.

But beware!

Mere athletic prowess won't be enough.

You'll need your wits as well.

Correctly answer two tricky riddle-questions

the python puts to you,

and you'll win this grand prize:

YOUR VERY OWN TEMPLE!

Artemis gasped. This was some prize! No wonder everyone seemed so excited. Noticing the asterisk at the end, her eyes automatically sought out the footnote at the bottom of the poster. She found this:

Warning: Winning will be harder than you think. Hundreds have already tried. And failed. Good luck to all athletes!

Underneath, someone had added four handwritten words: *But no girls allowed.*

She gritted her teeth, wondering which of the godboys had added *that* qualification. It wouldn't surprise her to find out it was Actaeon. But it could have been one of the giants, too. Or Ares. Or even Apollo if he'd been in the main hall before she saw him out in the courtyard.

"Wish I could enter," someone said wistfully. Artemis turned to find Medusa standing behind her. "Bet *I* could beat that python. Snakes don't scare me." The green girl reached up to stroke her snaky hair, and her reptiles twined fondly around her wrist like bracelets.

Talk about an unlikely ally! She and Medusa hardly ever saw eye to eye about anything. Of course, Artemis had no interest in this contest herself. She didn't really like tangling with beasts. But why shouldn't someone like Medusa, or, say, *Athena*—who was smarter than all the boys at MOA put together—be able to participate in such a contest of wits?

"You *should* be able to enter," Artemis said firmly.

Medusa gave her a guarded smile. "You think so?"

"Definitely," said Artemis. Someone had to stand up for the girls. It might as well be her! "It's not fair that we can't compete in the Games if we want to. And I'm going to go talk to Principal Zeus about it. Right now!"

4

Visiting Zeus

S TOP! YOU CAN'T GO IN THERE!" ALL NINE OF

Ms. Hydra's heads swiveled to look at Artemis as she

raced past the administrative assistant and burst into

Zeus's office unannounced.

Before she could lose her nerve, Artemis blurted in

a rush, "I have something important to say! It's about

the—" Suddenly she stopped, her shoulders drooping.

The golden throne behind the principal's desk was empty! Zeus wasn't even here. But then she heard his unmistakable booming voice.

"WHAT THE—?" he thundered in surprise. Whipping around, Artemis gasped when she saw him. Not because of his intimidating appearance, though that was terrifying enough since he was seven feet tall with bulging muscles, wild red hair, and piercing blue eyes. No, it wasn't that. It was because he was standing there with his feet braced wide, holding an entire four-drawer filing cabinet horizontally over his head. And he seemed poised to hurl it at her!

"MS. HYDRA?" he bellowed toward the door. "I THOUGHT I ASKED YOU NOT TO LET ANY- ONE INTO MY OFFICE UNTIL I FINISHED MY WORKOUT!"

Ms. Hydra's long-necked grumpy green head had followed Artemis and was poking through the doorway frowning at her. "Don't blame *me*. I tried to stop her, but she wouldn't listen!"

"It's important," Artemis repeated, clasping her hands anxiously.

Eyeing her, Zeus continued pumping the file cabinet up and down, muscles flexing. Then, he sighed deeply. "Oh, all right. It's okay, Ms. Hydra." As Ms. Hydra's head snapped back out the door, Zeus tossed the cabinet over his shoulder to crash-land on its bottom end a few feet behind him. *BOOM!*

"Take a seat," he said, pointing her toward a small chair in front of his desk as he headed around to his throne. Her chair's flowered cushion had a hole, where its stuffing poked out on the side. One of Zeus's little accidents, she supposed. He was always zapping stuff with electrical sparks that flew from the tips of his fingers.

As Artemis scooped discarded Thunder Bar wrappers and a gym towel off the chair seat so she could sit, she gazed around the office. Files, scrollazines, papyrus maps, and empty bottles of Zapple were scattered everywhere. Scorch marks from errant thunderbolts covered the walls.

Seeing her stare, Zeus added, "Something wrong?"

"Nope," she said honestly. Everything looked fine to her. After all, her dorm room wasn't any tidier!

Zeus stepped behind his desk and lowered himself onto his huge golden throne. "Now, what's this all about, uh—?" He glanced at her questioningly.

"Artemis," she supplied.

"Right. The archer," he said. Everyone knew that he wasn't good with names, so she wasn't offended he'd forgotten hers. And at least he'd remembered her skill with a bow and arrow. Suddenly leaning forward with his arms folded on top of the mass of papers on his desk, he pinned her to the chair with his intense blue eyes. "Well? Out with it! What's so important?"

Artemis gulped, staring at the wide, flat, golden bracelets that encircled his wrists. And the thunderbolt trophy on his desk that stood three feet tall. She squirmed in her chair. Now that she had his full attention, she didn't feel quite so sure of herself. It was hard to feel confident talking to someone who was not only principal, but King of the Gods and Ruler of the Heavens too! No one told Zeus what to do. No one. Not even Athena, and she was his daughter!

"I—um—" Artemis hesitated, trying to think how to phrase what she wanted him to do without making him mad.

He drummed his fingertips on the desktop impatiently. With each tap, sparks of electricity zinged from his fingers. A curl of smoke wafted upward from one of the papers. Before she could jump up and put the fire out, Zeus slammed his fist down, snuffing out the tiny flame. She wasn't sure he'd even noticed the paper was on fire. He was just annoyed. With her. *Gulp.*

"This is a busy week for me, you know!" he boomed. "With the Olympics going on. I don't have all day to shoot the breeze!"

"But that's exactly what I wanted to talk to you about," Artemis said quickly, fearing he might toss her out. "The Olympics."

Zeus lifted a bushy eyebrow. "Is there a problem?

Nothing I hate worse than bad sportsmanship, and I heard something about a scuffle out on the field." Eyeing her, he picked up the thunderbolt trophy from his desk and began pumping it with one arm. Artemis backed up a little in her chair, just in case the trophy accidentally slipped from his grasp. "Figured it was only a rumor, though, since the Games are meant to bring students together in harmony. Was I wrong?"

Uh-oh. She hadn't come here to rat on anyone. Especially since she was as much at fault as anybody for what had happened that afternoon. But it sounded like Pheme hadn't been able to stop herself from spreading the news. "You? Wrong?" she replied, pretending to be shocked at the very idea.

"It happens sometimes," Zeus said, shrugging modestly. "Not very often of course," he added quickly. "After all, I am King of the Gods!"

Artemis nodded and scooted forward in her chair, seeing an opening. "Did you by any chance hear another rumor? The one about girls wanting to participate in the Games?"

Zeus's eyes took on a puzzled look and he slowly lowered the trophy he'd been pumping. There was a terrible silence. Just when she thought she might be thunderbolted into smithereens for her boldness, he suddenly cracked a huge smile, his eyes twinkling merrily. "Oh, I get it. This is a joke, right? Okay, I'll bite. No, I didn't hear that one." He looked at her eagerly, waiting for her to tell him the punch line of her supposed joke.

"It's not a joke!" said Artemis. "Girls are good at sports too. Why shouldn't we be allowed to compete?"

Zeus looked confused. "Why would you want to? Think you could out-lift Atlas? Or wrestle a giant?"

"Well, no, but—"

"Didn't think so," interrupted Zeus, shaking his head. "There's a reason girls aren't in the Games. Because I, King of the Gods and Ruler of the Heavens, made a rule that they couldn't be."

"But—"

Zeus held out a hand to stop her, shaking his head. "It's for your own good. The Games are fierce, you know. You could get hurt. No, there are plenty of competitions girls are free to enter here at MOA, but the Olympics are and always will be a boys-only event." He folded his arms with finality, gold bracelets flashing.

Artemis wasn't giving up. This was too important. "Not all the events are about strength. What about the footraces? And this year's special event—the contest of wits with the Python?"

"I made my rule long ago, and I don't see any reason to change it. I still believe that the best way for you—for *all* girls—to enjoy the Games is from a seat in the bleachers." As if that settled things, he kicked back in his throne, unrolled an *Immortal Sports* scrollazine, and started to read. At the same time, he picked up his trophy again and began to pump it with his free hand.

"Knock, knock."

At the sound of a woman's voice, Artemis and Zeus both looked toward the door. Zeus immediately jumped up, dropping the trophy and scrollazine, a big smile on his face.

"Hope I'm not disturbing you," said a statuesque goddess with thick blond hair styled high upon her head. It was Hera, owner of Hera's Happy Endings, a wedding boutique in the Immortal Marketplace. She and Principal Zeus had been seeing a lot of each other lately. They'd met at the last school dance after Athena's mom, a fly named Metis who had lived inside Zeus's head, had flown off to be with her fly buddies.

"Come in," said Zeus, ushering her toward his desk. "Artemis was just leaving." He bent to sniff at a covered dish that Hera held in her hands. The delicious aroma of sweet nectar reached Artemis's nose. "For me?" he asked, sounding as excited as a little boy.

"MS. HYDRA, FETCH A SPOON!" he yelled out the door.

"Not yet," Hera said firmly. "It needs to cool." Bustling past him, she set the dish on top of his desk.

As Artemis rose from her chair and headed for the door, Hera peered at her appraisingly. Artemis glanced down at her chiton. It had dried stiff and wrinkled since her fall in the fountain. And her hair was probably straggly. She'd forgotten she was a mess! "You're Athena's friend, aren't you?" Hera asked.

Artemis nodded. Smoothing her chiton as best she could, she raked her fingers through her tangled hair. She wondered if Hera had caught much of her conversation with Zeus before she'd knocked. If so, she didn't mention it. Hera just smiled and said, "Nice to see you again."

"You too," said Artemis. And she meant it. After Metis left, Zeus had been in a horrible, stormy mood. The courtyard still bore the marks of the lightning bolts he'd rained down everywhere. His friendship with Hera had changed all that.

After leaving Zeus's office, Artemis zipped up to her room to change clothes. She guessed it was unrealistic to think she could get a long-standing tradition like the

Olympics changed just three days before the Games began. And Zeus had a point that girls might get hurt in events of strength against the boys. Besides, the boys had been training all year long and it was probably too late for the girls to catch up.

Hmm. *Too late to catch up.*

Suddenly it hit her. A way to fix things so they were fair. It was so simple, she didn't know why she hadn't thought of it before!

5

Zzzzing!

Y OU'LL NEVER BELIEVE WHERE I JUST WAS,"
Artemis said to her friends as she plunked her tray on
top of their usual table in the cafeteria.

Persephone glanced up at her, a forkful of nectaroni
halfway to her mouth. "Where?"

"In Principal Zeus's office." Artemis slid a plate

of ambrosia salad off her tray, then stuck a straw into her carton of nectar.

Athena dropped the textscroll she'd been skimming. "Are you in trouble?" she asked worriedly. "I *knew* Pheme wouldn't be able to keep her mouth shut about this afternoon. I'll talk to Dad if you want. I'll tell him Actaeon deserved what he got. Anyway, there was no harm done, and—"

"Stop!" exclaimed Artemis, holding up a hand. "I'm not in trouble. I went to his office on purpose!"

Her friends' jaws all dropped in astonishment. "Why?" Aphrodite asked. Even with her mouth hanging open, she still managed to look gorgeous with her long golden hair and her sparkling blue eyes.

Artemis swallowed a sip of nectar. "To convince him to let girls compete in the Olympics."

"Godness!" Aphrodite exclaimed. "Are you crazy?"

"What did he say?" asked Persephone.

Artemis shrugged, then answered both questions. "No. And no."

"Figures," said Athena. "The only ideas my dad likes are his *own*." She paused. "And maybe Hera's, too, these days."

"Well, on the way here I got another idea," said Artemis. "One he can't say no to."

"Uh-oh," said Aphrodite, only half-joking.

"His main argument against us competing was that we might get hurt in contact sports with the guys."

"He's got a point," said Persephone.

"Yeah, but I thought of a way around that," Artemis said. "We'll start a *girls-only* Olympics!"

There was a brief silence at the table.

"Well?" prompted Artemis. "No cheering? Where's

your enthusiasm?" First, Apollo wouldn't support her and now it looked like her friends wouldn't either!

Athena spoke up. "What makes you think my dad'll be okay with that?"

"Because we're not going to ask him," Artemis informed her. "We're just going to do it."

Athena looked uncertain.

"Well, I think it's a great idea," Persephone chimed in.

"Me too," said Athena. "I'm just not sure my dad will agree. And the Olympics are in three days. No way we can be ready by then."

"True. We'll need time to train, and to get word out about it to girls at other schools," Aphrodite said slowly. "It won't be much of a competition if we don't actually have some competition!"

Yes! thought Artemis. If Aphrodite was on board, she'd set an example for other girly-girls who might otherwise turn up their noses at a girls' games.

"We could probably be ready in a few months," mused Persephone. "If we hold our games at a different time from the boys', it won't take attendance away from their games. So they shouldn't mind, right?"

"Right," said Artemis. "And if they do mind, so what?"

"If Dad sees how committed we are, maybe he'll listen to reason," Athena said, sounding more enthusiastic.

Artemis hoped she was right. "It's worth a try." While the girls were agreeing to meet that night to begin making a game plan, she looked around for Apollo. Maybe his mood had improved by now. Maybe he'd even be ready to apologize for what he'd said to her! Unfortunately she didn't see him anywhere.

Out of the corner of her eye she glimpsed Actaeon,

sitting with his back to her, at a table with Hades and Poseidon. Apollo had called her behavior toward him "inexcusable." Now that she'd had time to cool off, she was beginning to think he might be right, and that she owed Actaeon an apology for turning him into a stag. Still, she wasn't quite ready to talk to him, especially not with other boys around.

When she went to empty her tray after dinner, Artemis ran into Dionysus, her brother's fun-loving roommate. "Do you know where Apollo is?" she asked.

"He was practicing his kithara when I left the dorm," Dionysus told her. Apollo was a master of the seven-stringed lyre, and his and Dionysus's band, Heavens Above, played for all the school dances. "He said he was going to skip dinner and go for a walk instead. Said he had some heavy thinking to do."

That's weird, Artemis thought. Like most boys,

Apollo was *always* hungry. Especially after sports. He *never* skipped a meal.

"Thanks," she told Dionysus. She headed toward the marble staircase to fetch her dogs for a walk. Maybe she could "accidentally" run into Apollo while she was out. She raced up the stairs to the fourth floor. As soon as she opened the door to her room, all three dogs leaped on her, wagging their tails. "Yes, we're going for a walk," she said, laughing. She threaded her way past a mountain of laundry, dog toys, and old discarded school projects to reach the far side of her room. After grabbing her favorite archery bow, she dug under a pile of textscrolls on top of her desk to unearth her quiver. "Okay, boys, let's go!" she called, as she slung the tooled leather quiver across her back.

Once outside the bronze doors of the Academy, Artemis squeezed her eyes shut and concentrated on seeing Apollo in her mind's eye. Slowly, she recited the chant she and Apollo had made up in childhood:

"Come, my twin, give me a clue–

a picture I can use to find you!"

They'd always been able to locate each other in this way—as long as the other twin was *willing* to be found. Soon a picture of a familiar forest swam into her head. Then something with eight legs, a shiny exoskeleton, and crablike claws scurried into her picture. A humongous scorpion! There was only one place to find those—in the Forest of the Beasts down on Earth.

So that was where Apollo had gone! Technically, students weren't supposed to go there except during their scheduled class time, but the Forest was only really off-limits to mortals. Still, what kind of idiot went there alone? The Forest could be dangerous—she knew that from personal experience! In Beast-ology classes, MOA students trained there sometimes, hunting mythical creatures like Minotaurs, Geryons—and scorpions, too, of course.

"Stay!" she commanded her dogs. Then she dashed back inside MOA and grabbed a pair of winged sandals from the big basket by the doors. Someone had left a bowl of snacks for the athletes on a table in the main hall, so she pocketed a few apples and fig bars. Knowing Apollo, he'd be hungry when she found him.

Once outside again, she slipped the sandals on. Their laces twined around her ankles and the silver wings at her heels began to flap. Soon she was speeding across the courtyard and down from Mount Olympus to the Forest. Her dogs raced after her, doing their best to keep pace.

When Artemis reached Earth, she slowed at the edge of the Forest to let her dogs catch up. Only a thin crescent moon lit the rapidly darkening sky. She'd need a torch to find her way. Pulling a silver arrow from her quiver, she blew lightly along the arrow's length to summon the moon's power. The feathers at one end of the arrow began to glow with a cool, bluish light that quickly zipped up the shaft to the arrowhead. Now the arrow was bright enough to light the evening path. Being the goddessgirl of the moon, as well as the hunt, had its advantages!

Quickly, she loosened her sandals' straps with her free hand and looped them around the silver wings, so that she could walk at a normal rate again. Holding the arrow-torch high in one hand, she moved through the Forest, her hounds trailing close behind her.

Now and then, the howling of some beast in the distance reached her ears. Despite her bravery, the sounds gave her goose bumps and also caused her dogs' ears to prick up. Just because she was goddessgirl of the moon and the hunt, that didn't mean she *liked* being out in the dark where beasts lurked. Of course, they weren't real beasts—only game projections created by her Beast-ology teacher—but they were scary just the same. And since things had gone dreadfully wrong with them once before, it could happen again.

Artemis glanced back at her dogs and saw Suez ("Zeus" spelled backward) lift his head to sniff the air. He growled deep in his throat. "What is it, boy?" she whispered. Then she spotted a creature with the body of a lion and the wings of an eagle, standing completely motionless not ten yards to her right. A Griffin! Though she knew the beast wasn't real—and at the moment it was even switched off—it still weirded her out. She and her dogs crept past the monster, going deeper into the woods. All was quiet until she stepped on a twig. *Snap!*

Zzzzzing! A golden arrow whizzed past her ear. As it zoomed by, it sang a line from a Heavens Above song: *We never will part, for you've pierced my heart!* Only Apollo had golden arrows that could sing! They were a gift from their friends on his last birthday.

"Ye gods!" Artemis cried, dropping to a crouch. "Stop, Apollo! It's me!"

It was a lucky thing he'd missed her. The arrow couldn't have actually hurt her since it had been dipped in the Pool of Magic, but even magic arrows stung when they struck.

"Artemis?" Apollo ran toward her, sounding worried. "What are *you* doing here?"

"Looking for you!" Artemis said grumpily, as she got to her feet. She waved her glowing arrow in front of his face. "Didn't you see me?"

"Sorry—I mistook you for a beast! This place always

makes me jumpy." Apollo didn't bother to ask how she'd known where to find him. He'd made use of their *twin sense* and chant to find her before too.

"Why are you here, then?" Artemis asked. Her dogs had leaped on him with joy as soon as he appeared. Now they were licking his face and hands as if they hadn't seen him in a hundred years, instead of only hours ago.

Apollo crouched to pat Suez on the head. Then he ruffled the fur on Amby's back with one hand and scratched Nectar behind his ears with the other. "I was—um—training my arrows?"

Artemis raised an eyebrow. "You didn't have to come here for that. You could've practiced with targets at MOA's archery field."

Apollo chewed at his lower lip, as if he was trying to think up another improbable excuse. "Um . . ."

"Don't bother. You're a lousy liar," Artemis told him, brushing off the dirt that still clung to her knees.

Apollo's shoulders sagged. "I know. It's a real curse." As the godboy of truth—and also of prophesy—he'd never been able to pull off a lie. "If you must know, I've been matching wits with the beasts. Bantering with them."

Artemis wrinkled her forehead. "Bantering with beasts? When they're turned off?"

Making a frustrated sound, Apollo said, "Not that it's any of your business, but I was practicing. You know, so I can defeat the Parnassus Python."

Artemis gaped at him in horror. "You're planning to enter the Python-o-thon?"

"Yeah, so?"

"So no offense, but you're horrible at riddles," she said. "I read that poster—Python's a serpent! One that could squeeze the breath out of you in less time than it takes to blink. It's not a fake beast-machine like the ones in this Forest!"

"See? This is why I didn't tell you," Apollo complained. "I knew you'd try to talk me out of it." Leaning down, he loosened the bindings on his sandals so their silver wings began to gently flap.

"Because it's a bad idea!" Artemis said, doing the same. She whistled to her dogs to follow, and they all took off through the Forest back toward the Academy.

"It's school rules that I have to compete in at least one event," said Apollo as they flew along, side by side. "And no matter what you think, I figure the Python-o-thon gives me my best shot at winning." He frowned, darting left to avoid a tree branch in their path. "If archery was part of the Olympics, I might win, but you're just as good at that as I am. I want to prove myself at something that doesn't involve you. I want to see what I can do on my own!"

Right behind him, Artemis went left too. Though she didn't like what he'd said, she understood. "The Python-o-thon is probably also going to require amazing strength," she warned.

"You mean like the strength Heracles has?" Apollo said sourly.

The path had widened, so Artemis moved alongside him and held her arrow-torch closer to study his face. "You can't really be jealous of Heracles, can you?" she asked. "He's only mortal. You're a *god*."

"'Course I'm not jealous!" he said, a little too quickly. "But you don't see heroic paintings of me decorating any temples around here. Heracles' feats are all over Principal Zeus's new temple!"

Artemis whipped around, flying backward for a

ways so she could face him. "So that's it! You want your own temple!"

Apollo stuck out his chin. "Maybe. Don't you?"

"Sure, but even if I *were* allowed to enter the contest, I wouldn't be crazy enough to do it. Not even for a temple!" Apollo was clever, but his inability to lie would put him at a real disadvantage with the wily serpent. Rumors were flying that it was as verbally devious as it was crushingly ruthless, and she did not want her brother going up against it!

"A temple means you've earned *respect*," he insisted. "And stop that—flying backward is dangerous."

Artemis whipped around to fly forward again. "You're a godboy. Respect goes with the territory," she went on. "Who are you trying to impress? Some girl?"

Apollo's face flushed. "No! Duck."

"Huh?" He was trying to impress a farm animal?

Apollo reached over mid-flight and tugged her into a crouch just in time to miss a low-hanging branch.

"Oh, that kind of duck. Thanks," said Artemis, straightening again.

"I'm not interested in girls right now. Not since—" He broke off, no doubt recalling how his very first crush had ended in disaster. To escape him, Daphne, a nymph huntress, had changed herself into a laurel tree instead of just telling Apollo she didn't like him back.

The forest nymphs were under Artemis's protection, and she'd hated to see that happen, but sometimes nymphs could be overly impulsive. What could you do? Thinking about Orion, her own disastrous first crush, she said, "You're not the only one who's unlucky in love."

A silence fell between them. As if to fill it, Apollo's stomach growled. "I'm starving," he muttered.

Remembering the apples and fig bars, Artemis slowed her pace. "Hold up. I brought you something to eat."

"Thanks," he said gratefully. Slowing as well, he took the snacks, devoured a couple of fig bars, then munched on one of the apples as they continued on.

"I didn't see you at dinner, so I figured you'd be hungry," Artemis said. "Good thing I brought something, huh?"

Apollo swallowed a bite of apple. "Look, Artemis," he said, his voice serious. "I appreciate the food. I really do. And I appreciate you watching out for me. You've always been the most loyal sister anyone could have. But—" He paused.

"But what?" Artemis asked.

He tossed the apple core over his shoulder. One of

her dogs caught it, then dropped it, probably disappointed it wasn't a bone. Apollo continued. "You've got
to stop being so—so *helpful*. Sometimes you act like you
think you're my mom instead of my sister!"

Artemis stared sideways at him through the dim
light of her arrow-torch. Feeling hurt, she wanted to
run away—to pretend this conversation had never happened. But that had never been her way.

Apollo ran a hand through his wavy black hair.
"Did you ever stop to think that sometimes I don't
want your help?"

"Then maybe you should give me that last apple
back!" Artemis snapped, reaching for it.

Grinning, Apollo held it away from her. "I meant no
help *after* this time." Quickly, he took a big bite of the
apple.

"Fine. I promise never to help you ever again." She expected that Apollo would utter a protest, and her heart sank when he didn't.

Soon the trail narrowed so they had to go single file. Apollo took the lead. By the time it widened, Artemis could see the lights of MOA up ahead. With her three hounds racing along behind, she and Apollo sped the rest of the way back to school in total silence. Almost like they were strangers!

6

Girls Only

ARTEMIS PULLED OPEN THE DOOR TO THE girls' dorm and started down the hall to her room. Panting hard, her dogs trailed behind her with their tongues hanging out. After racing to keep up on the return to MOA, they were exhausted. As soon as they got to her room, they trotted over to their water and food bowls. Within minutes, all three had flopped onto her spare bed and curled up for the night.

Seconds later, Aphrodite knocked and then opened the door to poke her head in. "We thought we heard you come back," she said. Persephone was right behind her. "We're in my room working on ideas for our girls-only games. Athena too. Are you coming?"

Persephone held up a chip, adding, "We've got snacks." Popping the chip in her mouth, she crunched it. At the sound, Artemis's dogs—who definitely knew the word "snacks"—suddenly perked up. Leaping off the bed, they slipped around the girls, and ran lickety-split for Aphrodite's room next door. The goddessgirls chased after them.

"No, Amby! Stop, Nectar! Down, Suez!" Artemis shouted as the snack-hounds dashed through Aphrodite's open door. Inside, Athena tried to save the bowls of chips and ambrosia dip, which had been sitting on the bed. But they wound up scattered on the floor. Aphrodite was the neatest person Artemis knew, so she did *not* look pleased.

Artemis grabbed the dogs and herded them back to her room. "Sorry about that," she apologized when she returned. "I love those dogs, but nothing gets between them and snacks!"

As the girls cleaned up the mess, Persephone looked at Artemis and asked, "Where've you been?"

"Yeah, you left the cafeteria in a hurry after dinner," Aphrodite added casually.

Artemis shrugged. "I needed to take my dogs out, so—"

"You sure were gone a long time," Aphrodite interrupted. She exchanged a look with Persephone and

Athena that Artemis wasn't sure how to interpret. "Did you have a nice walk?"

Flopping onto Aphrodite's spare bed now that things were cleaned up, Artemis sank into the plush red velvet comforter that covered it. "Yeah, I guess," she said, studying her friends. *What's going on here?*

Aphrodite examined her perfectly shaped, blue-polished nails. "You wouldn't have been meeting anyone on your walk, would you?"

Athena grinned, opening a new bag of chips. "Like a cute godboy, perhaps?"

All three girls look at her expectantly.

Godsamighty! thought Artemis, rolling her eyes. In her absence, they must have been concocting a romantic scenario that was as far from the truth of what had happened on her walk as the moon was from Earth. Sometimes her friends could be annoyingly boy-crazy.

Especially Aphrodite. Since she was the goddessgirl of love, that was to be expected, though.

Artemis reached for some chips. "How did you guess?" she said, stuffing a handful of them in her mouth. *Crunch!*

"I knew it!" Aphrodite crowed. "Who is he? Tell us!"

"Well," said Artemis, around a mouthful of chips, "He's tall, dark, and handsome."

"That description fits half of the godboys at MOA," Athena pointed out.

"Come on," coaxed Persephone. "We want a name."

Artemis swallowed, then took a swig of nectar, making them wait. "You sure?" she teased finally. "You might be disappointed."

Aphrodite gave her the stink eye. "Stop being so infuriating."

Artemis shrugged. "Okay, but don't say I didn't warn

you. The boy I was with just now was . . ." She paused for dramatic effect. "Apollo!" Then she rolled over on her side, laughing.

"Why, you—!" Realizing they'd all been had, Aphrodite threw a heart-shaped pillow at Artemis's head. She caught it and tossed it back, hitting Aphrodite in the chest. Soon all four girls were flinging pillows back and forth, while giggling up a storm.

When they finally calmed down, Athena said, "You're so lucky that both you and Apollo get to go to school here." Artemis wondered if Athena was thinking about Pallas—her best friend down on Earth. The one she'd had to leave behind when she came to MOA.

"Yeah, having a twin must be fun," Aphrodite said wistfully. She was born from sea foam, and had never even known her parents.

88

Persephone nodded. "You and Apollo are practically joined at the hip."

"Or more like at the brain," said Athena. "That mind trick you guys do to find each other is awesome."

"It does come in handy," agreed Artemis.

"Can you see him right now?" asked Persephone.

"Could if I wanted to, and if he let me."

"Does that mean—could Apollo see you with us now if he wanted to?" asked Aphrodite. She peeked at her reflection in her mirror to check her appearance, just in case.

"Can he hear us?" Athena asked in a hushed whisper. Suddenly her friends seemed a little creeped out by the whole mind thing they'd thought was so cool a minute ago.

"We can't hear each other," said Artemis. "And

we just get hints of what's going on. So Apollo could probably tell I'm with you guys. If he wanted to, like I said. And if I let him. Which I won't." She paused. "I'm a little better at it than he is. Maybe because I'm older—ten minutes older, but still."

Scooping a chip in the fresh bowl of ambrosia dip, Athena nodded, munching it. "You've always seemed like you're the big sister. The boss."

The goddessgirls laughed. All except Artemis, who couldn't help remembering Apollo saying, "Sometimes you act like you think you're my mom instead of my sister!" Was she too bossy around him? Not wanting to think about it, she changed the subject. "So, what ideas for our girl games have you gotten so far?"

"Ooh! Wait till you hear—I have the perfect event!" Aphrodite squealed, immediately forgetting about

Apollo. "We could have relay races where, instead of handing off a baton, we could pass off a little stuffed animal."

"Oh, that sounds *so* cute!" Persephone agreed.

Artemis squirmed. "I'm not so sure." She didn't want to hurt her friends' feelings, but wasn't the point of a girls-only Olympics to get boys to take female athletes seriously? That was *her* goal, anyway. Apollo had talked about wanting to earn *respect.* She was beginning to understand what he meant.

Unfazed, Aphrodite continued. "And for the long jump, we could have sparkly pink sand. Magic sand that would rise into the air and form a number at the end of each girl's jump to measure how far she went."

"I love it!" said Athena.

Artemis's uncertainty must have shown on her face

because, after a glance in her direction, Athena added diplomatically, "But maybe we should try to get support for our whole idea first before we decide on events. Dad might be more willing to consider a girls-only games if he knew lots of students were in favor of them."

"We could draw up a petition!" Persephone exclaimed.

"Good idea," said Artemis. Up until now, she hadn't been totally sure her friends were as interested in a girls' games as she was. Seeing their enthusiasm, she was sure other girls would like the idea too, as soon as they heard about it.

Aphrodite tapped her chin with a fingertip. "I wonder if we could come up with a better title than 'Girls-Only Olympics'? It's kind of a mouthful."

"I know! How about the 'Her-O-Lympics'?" Artemis suggested.

Her friends stared at her blankly.

"You know, 'Her'—as in female. Plus *O*. So it's a made-up word that's sort of like 'Hero,' only pronounced differently. And then you add 'Lympics.'"

"Um—" said Aphrodite.

"Well," hedged Persephone.

"You don't like it?"

"'Lympics' kind of sounds like 'limping,'" said Athena. "Not a good visual for a sports event."

"Any better ideas?" asked Artemis. The others were silent.

"Her-O-Lympics it is!" said Athena. "It'll do for now anyway."

"We can always change it later," agreed Artemis.

"Let's get going on that petition," said Athena. "Like I said, there won't *be* a Her-O-Lympics if we don't get enough support."

Aphrodite fetched her favorite red feather pen and several sheets of pink papyrus, and together the girls worked on the wording of the petition. When that was finished, Artemis made several copies of it, while the others made a big, bright poster. It read:

JOIN THE CAUSE:

HELP MAKE THE HER-O-LYMPICS A REALITY!

Aphrodite and Persephone decorated the poster with glittery hearts and flowers to make it stand out even more. Sports-themed decorations like balls and uniforms would've been more appropriate, thought Artemis, but she held her tongue.

When all was ready, they agreed to meet after school the next day to begin seeking signatures for their petition.

"Think we'll get any boys to sign it?" Artemis asked as they were heading off.

"I bet Hades will," said Persephone.

"So will Heracles," Athena said confidently.

Aphrodite frowned. "Ares may take some convincing, but he'll sign if he knows what's good for him!"

Artemis wanted to add that Apollo would sign. But would he? She'd always taken his support—his *loyalty*—for granted. But he'd been so prickly lately. Well, if he wouldn't sign the petition, she at least hoped he wouldn't work *against* them!

7

Big Giant Trouble

As ARTEMIS MADE HER WAY TO HER SECOND-
period Hero-ology class the next morning, her dogs
dashed and darted between sandaled feet in the hallway, playing their favorite game of Dodge-the-Student.
Suddenly, she heard yelling and scuffling up ahead.

"Yeah! Let him have it!" someone shouted. This was
followed by a loud *smack!*

"Whoa! That must've hurt!" someone else said in a half-admiring tone. Artemis stood on tiptoe to see over the students who had gathered around to watch the fight. But even on tiptoe she couldn't really see what was going on. "Stay!" she commanded her dogs.

After pushing through the crowd, she wasn't really surprised to find that Ares and Poseidon, egged on by some of the other godboys, were at it again with one of the giants. Fortunately, Apollo wasn't among the fighters or the eggers. His second-period class was in another wing.

What was this giant doing *inside* the Academy at all? Looking around, Artemis saw many other non-MOA athletes watching the fight too. Then she remembered that athletes were always invited to attend classes at MOA during the Games. She guessed it made sense, since they were missing classes at their own schools.

"You know, you *look* like a smart guy," Ares teased the giant. "What other impressions can you do?" Ares and most of the crowd laughed.

"Well, you don't even *look* like a smart guy," the giant retorted in the high, girly voice that belonged to Ephialtes. Either Ephialtes was horrible at jokes, thought Artemis, or she just didn't understand giant humor. His attempted joke fell flat.

"I'd say you're a pain in the neck," Ares quipped again, "but I have a much lower opinion of you!" His friends cracked up again.

Pushed too far by this second taunt, Ephialtes lunged. With a yelp, Ares sidestepped him, then threw a series of mock punches. Artemis tensed, watching the fight erupt. In the front office yesterday, Zeus had said, *"The Games are meant to bring students together in harmony."* Yeah, right! Some other students must have felt as uncomfortable as she did, because they tried to break things up. "Hey," said an MOA godboy named Eros, "can't we all just get along?"

But at the same time, Poseidon was creeping up behind the giant. "Yeah! Poke him in the butt!" someone yelled at the very moment Poseidon goosed Ephialtes with his trident.

The giant grabbed his rear with both hands and whirled around. "Why, you—!" Grabbing Poseidon around the waist, he lifted him over his head as easily as Zeus had lifted his file cabinet.

"Ow! Put me down!" yelled Poseidon as he bumped the ceiling.

"Yeah, put him down," said Ares, dancing around the giant and pretending to punch out at him like a prizefighter. "You know it's me you really want!" The giant only grinned at him, and began twirling

Poseidon overhead in one hand as he held Ares off with his other. Around and around Poseidon went, as if he were a baton and Ephialtes were a majorette.

"Yoo-hoo! Over here, giant!" Medusa called out, jumping up and down and waving from the back of the crowd. Hearing her, all the mortal students in the hall quickly put on stoneglasses. Just as sunglasses protected them from the sun, *these* glasses kept them from being turned to stone by Medusa's stare. Distracted, Ephialtes glanced her way.

She locked eyes with him, shooting him her infamous stare. But nothing happened! He just kept twirling Poseidon. Medusa's ability to turn someone to stone with a single glance worked only on mortals. And unfortunately for her, Ephialtes appeared to be immortal. If Artemis remembered her Histor-ology correctly, so were *most* giants.

Suddenly she wished Apollo was here after all. Then he'd see that she wasn't the *only* girl to stick up for a godboy. Medusa was trying to rescue Poseidon from this giant just like she herself had tried to rescue Apollo. But then, Medusa had been crushing on Poseidon for years. He was the one person Artemis had ever seen her be nice to!

All at once the floor began to shake. Artemis had wondered where the giant's twin had gotten to. Now here he was—thudding down the hall toward them. To avoid being trampled, the crowd split in two and squeezed back against the lockers lining both walls.

Just as Otus came to a stop, the door to the Hero-ology classroom was thrown open and Mr. Cyclops stormed out. "What in the name of Zeus is going on out here?" he demanded.

Except for Ares and Poseidon, all the other godboys

who'd been egging things on faded back into the wall-hugging crowd. Nodding toward Ares, Ephialtes roared, "He started it!"

"Did not!" Ares shouted back.

"Did too!" yelled Ephialtes.

"Did not!" Poseidon protested from his position above the giant's head.

Otus just stood there, like he was totally confused about what was going on.

Mr. Cyclops pointed at Ephialtes. "You—put Poseidon down." Then he pointed at Ares. "And you. Back off. I don't care who started this. It ends now." A vein in his forehead was pulsing and his humongous eye looked ready to pop out of his forehead. All three boys wisely shut up. Poseidon was set on the ground and Ares backed off. The hushed crowd waited to see what the teacher would do next.

Mr. Cyclops scowled at Ares. "Congratulations. You and Poseidon just won yourselves a date with Principal Zeus."

"But I—we—" Ares started to say. Mr. Cyclops pointed down the hall toward the principal's office. "Go!"

"Yes, sir," the two godboys said meekly at the same time. Ephialtes smirked.

As Ares and Poseidon trudged off down the hall, Artemis saw Ares glance over his shoulder at someone in the crowd. She followed his gaze and wasn't surprised to see Aphrodite returning his look with an encouraging smile. Had she seen who started the fight? Artemis wondered. Ares was hotheaded, but from what she'd seen of him so far, Ephialtes was too. The fight could just as easily have been the giant's fault.

Medusa sidled over to Artemis. "Mr. Cyclops is only siding with the giants because he's one too," she

103

muttered. Her snakes looked exhausted from all the excitement. They had tied themselves into a knot at the base of her neck, their sleepy-eyed heads trailing down her back like a dozen ponytails.

"Maybe, but he was on our side in the Titan War," Artemis reminded her. Histor-ology wasn't Medusa's best subject. "And Mr. Cyclops *would* be harder on Ares and Poseidon. The giants are guests here!"

"Whatever," muttered Medusa. She didn't seem too convinced.

Artemis had a feeling that Medusa would side with Poseidon no matter who was at fault. Still, she did feel sorry for Ares and Poseidon. It wouldn't be fun to be in their sandals when Principal Zeus heard about the fight. She hoped they were good at dodging thunder-bolts.

Mr. Cyclops's eye swept over the students still lingering in the hallway. "Show's over. Get to your classes."

As everyone started to scatter, the lyre bell sounded. "Second period will commence in five minutes," the school's herald announced in a loud, important voice.

Mr. Cyclops turned toward the giants. "As for you two, I'll see you both in my classroom at the end of the school day." From his tone of voice, it didn't sound like an invitation to a friendly little chat. *Good,* Artemis thought. The giants might be guests, but special treatment should only extend so far!

She whistled for her dogs to follow as she started toward the classroom door.

"Wait," said Medusa. "What happened with Principal Zeus?"

"Huh?" asked Artemis.

"You know. About girls getting to participate in the Python-o-thon?"

Artemis sighed. "Bad news. He said no. But," she added, her face brightening, "we're getting up a petition to start a Her-O-Lympics."

"A what?"

"A Her-O-Lympics."

"I heard what you said," Medusa replied. "I just don't know what it means."

Hmm, thought Artemis. Maybe, like her friends had hinted, her name for the Games *did* stink! "It's an Olympic Games for girls," she explained. "And the name is just temporary. We're open to suggestions."

"How about the Medusolympics?"

Artemis nearly burst out laughing, but then she saw that Medusa looked serious. "Um. Maybe," she hedged, starting for Mr. Cyclops's room. "Note it on the petition."

"Okay. Where is it?"

"Check for our table in the courtyard after school's out," said Artemis as she entered the classroom. Then she popped her head back out to add, "And be sure to spread the word."

Medusa nodded. "Later, then." As she headed off for her class, Artemis ducked back inside Mr. Cyclops's room.

She was surprised and a little alarmed to notice that one of the giant twins had followed her down the aisle to her seat. Her dogs didn't seem concerned, though. They just curled up on the floor around her feet.

After squeezing himself into the empty desk in front of her, the giant half-stood and turned toward her. *Wham!* His whole desk rose up with him, and then slammed back down on the floor. Artemis's dogs raised their heads and growled.

"Sorry, miss," the giant said in his deep voice. "Do

you want to trade places? I don't want to block your view of the board."

Artemis relaxed a little. So did her dogs. This was the friendly brother, Otus, thank godness. "No, that's okay. Mr. Cyclops might call on me less often if he can't see me," she said, only half-joking.

The giant flashed white teeth. He seemed a lot less scary when he smiled. The second lyre bell hadn't sounded, so she kept on chatting. "You're Otus, right? Ephialtes' brother?"

Otus, nodded, his eyes twinkling. "And you're Artemis, yes? The girl with the magic touch!"

Artemis blushed. He had to be thinking of how she'd turned Actaeon into a stag yesterday. "Yeah. Only I wouldn't have used my magic if I'd known what your brother's reaction would be."

Otus laughed. "If there's one thing my brother can't

resist, it's a hunt," he said. "He'd even abandon a pile of gold or, better than that, one of my mom's home-cooked meals to chase a stag."

Artemis smiled. "I have a twin brother too—Apollo. We're not identical twins like you and Ephialtes, though."

"Ephialtes and I *used* to be identical," Otus corrected. "But not anymore. See this?" Bending toward her, he rubbed his finger over a thin white scar above his left eyebrow. "A while back during a wrestling match, my head collided with my brother's teeth."

"Ye gods," she said, thinking maybe Zeus had it right when he didn't think girls should be wrestling the boys. "That must've hurt."

"Ephialtes got the worst of it. His tooth cracked and fell out, so now he's got a gap here." He pointed to a tooth in the middle of his bottom row of teeth.

From the corner of her eye, Artemis noticed that several students were frowning at her. Because she was talking to the enemy? She returned their scowls. She could talk to whoever she wanted! But just then the *ping, ping, ping* of the herald's lyre bell sounded, and Mr. Cyclops began to speak.

"Later," Otus whispered. With another *wham!* he swiveled in his desk to face the front of the room.

When class finally ended, he waited for her, blocking the aisle with his huge frame so that students had to find another route to exit the room. "I was wondering if you'd like to come watch my brother and me at wrestling practice in the arena tonight," he said.

"Thanks, I'll think about it," she said, but only to be polite. Watching a bunch of boys grappling and grunting in a wrestling match was not her idea of a good time.

"Oh, okay," he said, drooping a little at her hesitation.

"It's seven o'clock if you can come." She felt kind of sorry for him as she watched him lumber out of the room and down the hall. Though she didn't care much for Ephialtes, Otus was nice. For his sake, she hoped the two brothers would be able to keep out of any more trouble till the Games were over.

Why did he single me out? she suddenly wondered. Was he just anxious to have *one* friend here at MOA? Or was he crushing on her? She wasn't good at figuring boys out, but she certainly hoped it wasn't the latter!

8

No Fair!

O H, THIS IS SO AWFUL! WHERE'S APHRODITE?
Is she with Ares in his hour of need?" Persephone asked
worriedly as she took a seat next to Artemis at lunch-
time. They were the first to arrive at their table.

Artemis stared at her in surprise, wondering what
she was talking about. As Persephone set down her tray,
an ambrosia muffin bounced off her plate and rolled

onto the floor. All three of Artemis's dogs dove for it.

Persephone was so upset, she didn't even notice. "I heard that those giants broke both of Ares' legs and he had to be carried to the front office so Zeus could heal him in time for the first footraces." She glanced around the cafeteria as if planning to go give the giants a piece of her mind.

"No way! Where did you hear that?" asked Artemis. She looked for the giants too. Lucky for them, they weren't around. But Pheme was. The goddessgirl of gossip was in supercharged mode. Words puffed from her orange-glossed lips as she flitted from table to table, spreading rumors about the morning's big fight.

"Did Pheme tell you that?" she asked Persephone.

"No, but I overheard her telling someone else." Persephone hesitated. "Are you saying it's not true?"

Artemis nodded. "No!"

"Then you're saying it is true?"

"No! I mean yes. I mean it's *not* true. I was there. And Pheme wasn't."

"Well, that's a relief!" said Persephone, looking more relaxed.

"Actually, part of it's true," Artemis allowed. "Ares *did* go to Principal Zeus's office, but no one had to carry him. And as far as I know his legs are fine." *Though maybe someone should've examined his head,* she almost added, *because if he'd had any brains he wouldn't have gotten into a fight in the first place.*

She didn't say this last part however, because she caught sight of Actaeon just then. Seeing him reminded her of her own rash actions in what Aphrodite had since dubbed "the stag incident." (Although Aphrodite also thought the Trojan War she'd accidentally caused was only an "incident"!) Actaeon was balancing an empty tray in the lunch line, while the eight-armed lunch lady dished up bowls of yambrosia and handed them out to eight students at once.

Keeping an eye on him, Artemis blew on her spoonful of stew before having a bite. Apollo had called her actions toward Actaeon inexcusable. But Athena thought the boy deserved what he got. Artemis couldn't decide who was right. Whenever she softened and made up her mind to apologize, she remembered how Actaeon had pushed her into the fountain. And how he'd laughed at her!

Just thinking about it made her mad all over again. She scowled as he made his way toward a table, carefully holding up his lunch tray. He must have felt her gaze on him, because he glanced her way. As if the mere sight of her frightened him, he tripped and dropped his tray. His bowl of yambrosia flew off and landed upside down on the floor. It took Artemis several seconds to realize the accident hadn't been because of her after all. Someone had bumped him from behind when he'd paused.

"Smooth move, Actaeon!" hooted Atlas. The godboys at his table laughed. Other students craned their necks to look. Instead of getting mad, Actaeon grinned and bowed low from the waist. "And for my next trick," he said, "I will produce a *second* bowl of yambrosia." As everyone laughed with him, he started back to the lunch line.

By now Aphrodite had joined Artemis and Persephone at their table. "Poor Actaeon," she commented. "He hasn't had much luck lately."

"Meaning what?" Artemis said defensively. Until now her friends had mostly avoided discussing what she'd done to him, probably guessing rightly that it wasn't something she wanted to talk about.

"Never mind," Aphrodite said, dipping her spoon into her yambrosia. "It's just that—" She hesitated.

Artemis shot her a look. "It's just that what?"

Aphrodite shrugged. "I always thought he liked you. And I'm usually right about things like that."

"So did I," said Persephone.

Apollo had said the same thing, Artemis remembered. "Funny way to show it—pushing me into the fountain," she said.

"It could've been an accident," Persephone said softly. "I mean there was a fight going on. Someone might've pushed him into you."

"Yeah, sort of like what just happened with his tray." Aphrodite nodded her head toward Actaeon's upside-down bowl on the floor. A froggy-looking lunch lady, who was in charge of cleanup, had hurried over to deal with the mess. Unrolling her long, sticky tongue, she quickly and efficiently slurped up the spilled yambrosia. *Ick.* Artemis pushed her own bowl away, her appetite suddenly gone.

"He still shouldn't have laughed," she muttered. To be fair, she probably *had* looked funny with her hair dripping in her eyes and a magic fish flopping on her head. If it had happened to someone else, she might've laughed too! But she didn't want to admit she might've been wrong, even a teeny bit. "Let's talk about something else."

"Is it true what I heard about Poseidon fighting that giant today?" Athena said, arriving at the table just then.

Artemis groaned and dropped her head into one hand. "Not the kind of topic I had in mind."

"If the source was Pheme, I doubt it," said Persephone. "What did you hear?"

"No, I heard it from Pandora. She told me Poseidon single-handedly rescued Ares from the giants' clutches." Pandora was Athena's mortal roommate. She talked in questions, so Artemis figured what she actually said probably went something like this: *Poseidon? He–like–rescued Ares from the giant?*

"Ha!" said Aphrodite. "Something must be wrong with Pandora's stoneglasses. They not only blocked out Medusa's stone-gaze, but reality as well. Ares can take care of himself."

"Besides," added Aphrodite. "Pandora *would* believe a heroic story about Poseidon. She and Medusa have both been crushing on him for years."

Poseidon *was* cute—Artemis would give him that. But in her humble opinion, he was also kind of a drip— literally! His feet made squelching sounds when he walked, and he left wet footprints wherever he went.

No, if she had to pick a guy to crush on it would be someone like . . . like . . . She blinked as an image of Actaeon with his inquisitive gray eyes and light brown hair entered her head. Ye gods! She shook her head to clear it.

Then she and Aphrodite told the other two girls what *they* had actually seen during the fight. Their stories were pretty much in agreement, except that Aphrodite made Ares out to be kind of a hero. This surprised Artemis, but maybe Aphrodite really saw him that way. He was her crush, after all.

When lunch was over, and the girls were leaving the cafeteria, Artemis reminded them, "Don't forget to meet in the courtyard after school's out so we can set up our tables and petitions!"

Later that day, she met Aphrodite in the hall and walked with her to their last class—Revenge-ology.

Their teacher, Ms. Nemesis, usually stood at the door to greet everyone as they entered, but she wasn't there today.

Instead, the first thing they saw when they went inside was one of the giants. He was across the room talking to Atlas. When he laughed at something Atlas said, Artemis noticed the gap in his teeth where a tooth was missing.

"Looks like one of the giants is making friends," said Aphrodite. "I wonder which one he is?"

"Ephialtes," said Artemis.

Aphrodite cocked her head. "How can you tell?"

"He's missing a tooth. Otus told me."

"You talked to one of them?" She stared at Artemis in surprise, like she thought that was a daring thing to do.

Artemis shrugged. "Otus was in my Hero-ology class

this morning. He's nice, actually. Ephialtes is the hot-headed one."

Just then, Hera walked into the room, drawing every-one's attention as she went to the front of the classroom. She didn't bother to introduce herself, probably know-ing it wasn't necessary. By now everyone at MOA—even the athletes from other schools—knew who she was and had seen her with Principal Zeus.

"Ms. Nemesis has been called away this afternoon, and Principal Zeus has asked me to substitute," she announced. Reaching up, she smoothed a lock of blond hair that had escaped her perfect hairdo. She was so beautiful, she could almost be Aphrodite's mom, thought Artemis.

"Since your teacher's absence was unexpected, she didn't have time to brief me on her planned discus-sion topic. So I've decided that, today, we'll consider the concept of *fairness*." She smiled, her eyes twinkling. "I thought it might make for a more interesting discussion if we talk about the concept in terms of a current situation—say, the upcoming Olympic Games?" For some reason, she looked right at Artemis as she said it.

"You mean, do we think it's fair that giants are here for the Games?" a godboy called out from the back of the room. "I vote no!"

Artemis glanced at Ephialtes, half-expecting him to leap out of his desk—or shake it off, maybe, since he was wedged in there pretty tight—and go after the boy. Although he scowled, he managed to restrain himself. His expression relaxed when Hera spoke sternly to the godboy, "*All* of the athletes here from other schools are our guests. You would do well to remember that."

She paused to let that sink in, and then returned to her discussion subject. "The fairness issue *I* was thinking of concerns half of the students at MOA. And at some of our current guests' schools, too, I imagine. Can anyone guess who and what I'm referring to?" She looked straight at Artemis again, and suddenly Artemis knew why. Hera must've overheard some of her talk with Principal Zeus!

Artemis's hand shot up in the air. "You're referring to girls! To whether it's fair that we can't compete in the Olympic Games! And I vote that it's *unfair!*" Immediately, a hubbub erupted as everyone reacted to her statement at once.

Although Ephialtes shot her an annoyed look, he didn't join in the clamor. That was surprising since he had such strong feelings about girls even *watching* the Games. But then his glance turned snooty, as if he didn't even think it worth his time to *argue* with a girl!

"One at a time, please," said Hera. She called on Atlas.

"Why would girls want to compete with this?" Grinning, he flexed his biceps, showing off his muscles. "They'd get creamed!"

"*Yeah!*" chorused almost all of the boys. "You tell 'em!"

Artemis glanced at Apollo. He was nodding, the butthead. Did he really agree with them? Of course it was true that no girl would have a chance in a contest of strength against Atlas. He was the strongest godboy at MOA! Duh. But there were other sports girls excelled at.

Aphrodite flipped her long golden hair over one shoulder. The mere motion bedazzled the boys sitting nearby. Their cheering ebbed as their eyes went all goo-goo over her. "Really?" she asked. "Then which one of you—not counting Apollo—would like to challenge

Artemis to an archery contest?" Not one boy took up the challenge, knowing they'd lose.

Leaning across the aisle, Artemis high-fived Aphrodite. "You go, goddessgirl!"

From the back of the room a beefy-looking godboy named Kydoimos, called out, "Archery is not an Olympic event. How far can you throw a discus, Artemis?"

"I wouldn't know," she called back. "I've never been given the chance to try."

Suddenly arguments filled the room, as everyone wanted to have a say. Some of the girls in class giggled unsurely, while others shouted, "Yeah, Artemis is right. We deserve a chance!"

Hera called for order again. "Let's give the floor to the boys for a minute. I'd like to hear their major objections to girls' participation in the Games."

Artemis glanced at Apollo, willing him to come to

her defense—to the defense of *all* girls. She craved his support so much that when he raised his hand to speak, she smiled at him, sure he would tell the other boys they were wrong.

But instead, he said, "Girls can't compete with us. They'd get hurt! And that's that." Avoiding Artemis's eyes, he dusted his hands together as if the matter was settled.

Artemis wasn't about to let him know how much he'd hurt her. "No problem!" she countered hotly. "We'd rather have our own Games and choose our own events. Events more awesome than any *you* could ever have!"

A godboy named Makhai squinted his eyes at her and sneered. "Like what, cheerleading?" The boys laughed uproariously, and Ephialtes joined in with a high-pitched giggle.

In a voice full of outrage, Stheno, one of Medusa's

two sisters, spoke up. "Cheerleading takes a lot of stamina. Half the boys at MOA couldn't hack it!"

"That's right!" yelled the girls.

Before things could get too out of hand, Hera broke into the discussion again. "Remember," she said calmly, "the issue is *fairness.* Can anyone offer a definition of the term?"

"Something is fair if it's in accordance with the rules," offered Atlas.

"And the rules say the Olympics are for guys only!" added Kydoimos.

"But doesn't fairness also mean not showing favoritism to one group over another?" a girl named Aglaia asked, glancing at Hera.

Hera nodded. "Yes, that's another definition."

"And the rules for the Olympic Games favor boys," said Aphrodite. "So the rules are unfair!"

Apollo shrugged. "Rules are rules. And Principal Zeus made them. Deal with it!"

"Yeah! Rock it, Apollo!" the boys called.

Artemis's eyes flashed. "Don't worry. We *will* deal with it! Just you wait."

The girls cheered. "You tell 'em, Artemis!" yelled a goddessgirl with large pink wings, who Artemis barely knew. "We should have our own Games! Who needs boys?"

The godboys laughed, and so did Ephialtes. "Dream on!" one of them told her.

Ooh! They are so annoying! Artemis didn't want Hera to find out about the petition yet, in case she told Zeus and he called a halt to their plans before they could even start them. But before she could stop herself, she said, "It's not just a dream! Come on out to the courtyard after school, and you'll see!"

She couldn't wait to see the expressions on these boys' faces when they discovered what she and her friends had planned. To tell the truth, she'd been a little worried that some of the girls, especially the nonathletic ones, wouldn't care enough to sign a girl-Games petition. But the discussion in Revenge-ology today had given her cause an unexpected boost. It was almost as if Hera was on their side and had stirred up this controversy on purpose. Not only that, but Pheme was in the back of the room taking it all in. The news of the boys' unfairness would be all over school within the hour. What a stroke of luck!

9
Gathering Dignatures

As SOON AS REVENGE-OLOGY ENDED, ARTEMIS AND
Aphrodite dropped off their stuff in their lockers.
Then they hurried to the cafeteria to borrow tables
to set up in the courtyard, where they could catch students going to and from the school. "Need some help?"
asked a couple of godboys who'd come by for a snack.
Aphrodite was a magnet for boys' offers of help.

"Sure," said Aphrodite. She pointed to several tables folded up against a wall. "If you could just carry two of these to—" She hesitated, and then a look of determination came over her face. "Thanks anyway, but we can do it ourselves."

"You sure?" asked one of the boys doubtfully. "They're awfully heavy."

"And we're awfully *strong*," Artemis said with emphasis.

The boys were right, though. The tables *were* heavy. And Artemis's dogs were no help. They bumped up against the girls' legs, and squeezed back and forth under the first table as the girls struggled to get it out through the Academy's front doors.

Fortunately, Persephone and Athena arrived just then with the petitions and the poster they'd made.

Aphrodite and Artemis quickly filled them in on what had gone on in their class with Hera as substitute. With all four of them working together, it didn't take long to get a second table and four chairs down the granite steps and set up in the courtyard.

"I sure hope this works," said Persephone as she propped their JOIN THE CAUSE poster on an easel near the tables.

"It will," said Artemis, feeling confident. But at the same time, a tiny worry zinged through her brain. What if Principal Zeus saw them? She wasn't really defying his orders, since she wasn't trying to join the boys' games. Still, he hadn't given them permission to try and start their own. In fact his exact words had been, ". . . *the best way for you—for all girls—to enjoy the Games is from a seat in the bleachers.*" Didn't he realize how belittling that was? Their petitions just *had* to make him change his mind!

As the girls took their places behind the tables, Artemis's three hounds settled in the shade under the chairs. Armed with their four pink papyrus petitions and pens, the goddessgirls waited for "customers." It wasn't long before a couple of girls wandered over. "What's this all about?" asked a young goddess in a purple-flowered chiton. A wreath of purple crocuses sat atop her head.

"We're gathering signatures to convince Principal Zeus to let us girls hold our own Olympics," Artemis explained. "Want to sign our petition?"

"Hey," said the second girl, whose chiton shimmered with all the colors of the rainbow. "We talked about how unfair it was that the Olympic Games are boys-only during lunch!" She frowned. "I wanted to slug this godboy who said he could just imagine the dumb events girls would want to add."

"What were they?" Athena asked.

"I don't remember all of them, but one suggestion was speed fingernail-painting."

"That is so ridiculous!" scoffed Aphrodite. But then she looked thoughtfully at her own sparkly pink nails which, Artemis recalled, had been blue yesterday. "On the other hand," Aphrodite joked. "That's an event I might just have a chance at winning!"

They all laughed. "Where do we sign?" asked the first girl. Artemis and Persephone quickly shoved their petitions and pens across the table. The girl with the purple crocus wreath took Artemis's green feather pen and signed her name—*Antheia*—with a flowery flourish. The other girl borrowed all four pens so she could print her name—*Iris*—using a different color for each letter.

"I wish we could ask Hera to sign," said Athena, once they'd gone.

Artemis shook her head. "Zeus might find out. We need a *bunch* of signatures to show him before that happens."

Just then Medusa and her sisters, Stheno and Euryale, marched up to the tables. "Give us some pens!" Medusa said in her usual bossy manner. "We're signing!" For once the goddessgirls were happy to do as she requested. Aphrodite, Athena, and Persephone eagerly shoved their petitions and feather pens toward the three girls. As she was signing her name on Aphrodite's petition, Medusa pushed down so hard that the tip of her pen punched a hole in the papyrus. A look of embarrassment flitted across her face.

"No problem," Aphrodite said smoothly. She flipped the petition over. Touching a fingertip to the hole, she used a bit of magic to instantly mend the tear. "See, all better now."

Quickly recovering from her embarrassment, Medusa said, "Hmph. You should've used thicker papyrus!" After she finished signing her name, she and her sisters flounced off.

The goddessgirls looked at one another. "Whatever," said Persephone, which made them all laugh.

Before long, girls were lining up to sign. Artemis gleefully watched the signatures on her petition add up. She had fifteen already, including Aglaia's and Pandora's. If the others had about as many, that made *sixty*! She wondered how many girls attended MOA. She was about to ask Athena, who was likely to know, when some girls in line started to giggle. Glancing up, she saw that a boy had sneaked into her line.

"Hi, Artemis," said Actaeon. "How's it going?"

Artemis felt her heart beat faster. Hardening it against him, she said coolly, "You here to make fun of me again?"

Grinning, Actaeon flattened both hands on his chest, acting surprised at the idea. "Are you kidding? I wouldn't dare. You might turn me into something even worse than a stag!"

Artemis couldn't help smiling back. "Like what? Just in case you annoy me again and I need some ideas."

His grin widened. "Hmm. Next time I think I'd like to be something flashier. Maybe a Geryon?"

Artemis brushed the feathery tip of her pen on her chin, pretending to consider. "I think I'd go for something less daunting. Maybe a toad?"

He burst out laughing. "A toad? Give me a break!" Just then, Suez wiggled out from under the table and pushed his head against Actaeon's leg. "Hey, boy."

Actaeon reached down to ruffle the fur on the hound's neck. "You think maybe I should ask her to turn me into a dog next time?" The girls behind him drifted over to Athena's line, when they saw he was going to hang around and chat. Suddenly, Actaeon straightened. His eyes looked into hers. "Listen," he said solemnly, "I want you to know that I—"

But before he could finish, some athletes came along on their way back from the sports fields. Pointing at the girls' poster, one of the boys grabbed his stomach and pretended to laugh like crazy. "Olympic Games for girls? Ha-ha-ha!"

Artemis recognized only two of the four boys—Makhai and Kydoimos—but all had skin that shimmered slightly, which meant they were immortals. "I can guess whose dumb idea this is," Kydoimos said, jerking his thumb toward her. He snatched up her petition, running an eye over the list of names. "You haven't gotten one single boy to sign—not even your own brother!" He tossed the petition down disdainfully.

Artemis searched her mind for a great comeback. Before she could come up with anything, a voice said, "'Scuse me, can I borrow a pen?" It was Actaeon!

"No way!" said Makhai, practically having a fit as Actaeon stepped closer to the table. "You're not going to turn traitor on us, are you?"

"Yeah, we guys have to stick together," added Kydoimos.

Artemis pushed the petition toward Actaeon, daring him. Aphrodite held out a pen. The goddess-girls held their breath as they waited to see what he would do.

Actaeon hesitated for a few seconds. Then, taking the petition, he quickly signed his name.

"Woo-hoo!" Athena cheered.

"Our hero!" crowed Aphrodite.

"Arghh!" one of the other boys moaned, as if he were dying.

"I can't believe you just did that! Girls and Olympic Games don't mix," said Makhai.

Boom! Boom! The girls' pens bounced on the tables as a giant loped toward them. Seeing him coming, Kydoimos muttered, "Just like gods and giants don't mix."

A giant shadow fell over their table. Artemis glanced up at the scar on the giant's forehead. *Otus!* Quickly reading the sign, he bent and picked up a pen. It looked like a toothpick between his big fingers as he signed his name on Artemis's petition. Then he stood and glared at the boys. "Why don't you all *mix* yourselves on outta here?"

Makhai shrugged. "Big deal. Signatures from a mortal, and a giant who doesn't even go to school here. I still don't see any godboys signing! Come on, guys." With that, the four immortals took off, snobbish looks on their faces.

"So . . . are you up for wrestling tonight?" Otus asked Artemis, as the other goddessgirls began discussing what had just happened.

"Um, I don't know," said Artemis, only half-listening as she tried to tune into her friends' conversation too. "I think you might squash me, don't you?"

The thin white line above Otus's eyebrow shifted upward as he grinned. "I meant are you up for *watching* some wrestling. The practice match I told you about is tonight, remember?"

"Oh, right." Sighing inwardly, she said, "Okay, I'll be there." She owed him one for adding his name to the petition, after all. Speaking of owing someone, where was Actaeon? She looked around, but he'd disappeared.

As more girls arrived, Otus took off too. "Awesome! See you!"

"Thanks for signing!" Persephone called after him. "Yeah!" Artemis added.

All four goddessgirls were buzzing with excitement now. Every time another girl came to sign, or another boy made fun of them, they quickly pointed out the two boy signatures they'd already gotten. Who cared if they weren't from immortal boys? They were still from boys. But though they got plenty of girl signatures, no more boys would sign.

That night during dinner, Artemis watched for Apollo in the cafeteria, but he didn't turn up. *Godsamighty!* Where was he? She wanted to find out where she stood with him, especially after what he'd said in Revenge-ology. Had his loyalty shifted from her to his friends now? Or would he support her and sign the petition?

After saying good-bye to her friends, she spoke the twin chant under her breath, searching for Apollo with her mind. Only she couldn't come up with a clear image of his whereabouts. Was he blocking her? *Grr.* Sometimes brothers could be so annoying!

Well, she didn't have time to look for him now. She'd promised to go watch Otus wrestle. Leaving her dogs to nap in her room, she set off for the outdoor arena where the practice was taking place.

As she entered the circular arena, Artemis was surprised to see Athena sitting three rows up in the stands. But then she saw her wave at Heracles, who was seated on the athletes' bench at the edge of the arena, and knew she'd come to support him. Coach Triathlon was there too. And, *gulp*, Principal Zeus. Had he heard about the petition? Quickly she ducked into the stands and went to sit by Athena.

Elbowing her, Artemis gestured to where the principal sat. "Do you think your dad knows what we're up to?"

Athena shook her head. "No, I talked to him a minute ago, and he didn't mention it." Before they could discuss it further, a cheer went up from the crowd. The wrestlers were coming out onto the floor of the torch-lit arena. Artemis counted eight of them: Heracles, Atlas, Otus, Ephialtes, and four wrestlers she didn't know from other schools. The boys began to warm up with stretches.

"Who is Heracles up against?" Artemis asked.

"Otus," said Athena. "I'm a little worried. Even

though Heracles is strong, a giant is . . . well, giant!"

"Otus won't hurt him. I don't think."

Athena shuddered. "I'm just glad Heracles won't be in the ring with Ephialtes. Those giants may be twins, but they aren't much alike personality-wise, are they? I can't see Ephialtes signing our petition!"

Artemis nodded. "Me either." *And he probably wouldn't be any too happy if he knew his brother had signed it,* she thought. She wondered if Otus had told him.

Heracles and Otus's match was first. Before they began, they looked up at the girls and waved. Then they faced off against each other, looking serious.

Athena leaned closer. "Know much about wrestling?" she asked as Otus grabbed Heracles around the waist and lifted him in the air.

"Nope," Artemis admitted.

"That's called a *throw* for obvious reasons," said

Athena as Otus tossed Heracles toward the mat. He landed on both feet and moved quickly behind Otus. Reaching high, he grabbed the giant around the chest and pulled him backward toward his own chest. Though Otus was much taller and larger, Heracles was proving just as strong.

"Wouldn't it be easier just to trip him?" Artemis asked.

"Tripping's against the rules," said Athena. "You can't grab your opponent below the waist or hook his leg."

"I see," said Artemis, intrigued now. There was more to wrestling than she'd realized. She guessed it shouldn't have surprised her that Athena knew so much about it. Whenever her brainy friend got interested in a subject, she immersed herself in it, learning all there was to know.

"The object is to pin your opponent's shoulders to the mat and hold him down for at least three seconds," said Athena as Otus broke free from Heracles' hold.

When the match was over, Artemis was surprised to learn that Heracles had won, since neither he nor Otus had managed to pin the other. "It's because he scored more points for the moves he made than Otus did for his," Athena explained.

The boys shook hands good-naturedly, and then went to sit on the athletes' bench. Artemis was glad to see that they got along even in a competition.

Ephialtes and Atlas were up next. As they began to grapple with each other, Hera appeared by the bleachers. A huge smile lit up Zeus's face, and he waved her over. Just then, Ephialtes grabbed Atlas from behind and swung him up over his head as if the godboy weighed less than that giant tooth Ephialtes had lost. Beaming a smile, he spun Atlas around twice before tossing him to the mat.

"Atlas is losing, isn't he?" said Artemis. "Your dad's not going to like that."

The girls peered down at Zeus and Hera, but it didn't look like they were paying much attention to the match right now. From the way they were waving their hands around, it appeared their conversation was a heated one. Suddenly Hera frowned. Crossing her arms, she shook her head at Zeus emphatically.

"Whoa," said Athena. "Are they fighting?"

Zeus said something to Hera. Even though the girls couldn't make it out, there was no mistaking his sharp tone. She stood up as if to leave, but whatever Zeus said next must have changed her mind because then she sat back down. Zeus put his arm around her shoulders and she whispered something in his ear.

"Phew," said Artemis. "I guess it wasn't a big deal."

"Guess not," said Athena, relaxing. "She's made Dad so happy. I'd hate to see things go back to how they were before he met her."

"Everyone at MOA would hate that," Artemis said sincerely. "Things were pretty bad around here after your mom buzzed off."

"Yeah, no kidding!" Athena agreed. After Metis had gone, Zeus's constant grouchiness had clouded everyone's mood. "I wonder what they were arguing about."

Artemis shrugged. "Who knows?" Their eyes were drawn back to the match when they heard a big *thump*. Ephialtes had tossed Atlas onto his back and pinned his shoulders to the mat, thus winning the match. He jumped to his feet, grinning, and then did a quick victory lap around the mat.

"Show-off!" muttered Athena.

As Ephialtes finished his lap, Atlas got to his feet. He held out his hand to offer his congratulations. Which was the sportsmanlike thing to do of course. Ignoring him, Ephialtes pumped his fists in the air. "I'm number one!" he shouted. Poor Atlas, who had been friendly to the giant in Revenge-ology class earlier, slowly lowered his hand. Looking embarrassed, he shuffled off to the athletes' bench.

"What a bad sport!" Artemis huffed as the giant finally went to sit on the bench too.

"You can say that again," said Athena. "I'm just glad Dad didn't see."

As Artemis glanced toward Zeus and Hera again, she saw they only had eyes for each other. Zeus said something that made Hera laugh, and in return, she kissed him lightly on the cheek.

Athena sighed in delight. "Aw, how sweet."

Although she usually gagged over mushy stuff, Artemis nodded in agreement. She was glad Zeus was happy. Because when he was unhappy, it rained thunderbolts at MOA!

10
Keep Away

HALFWAY THROUGH THE NEXT MATCH,
Artemis nudged Athena, "I'm going to go find Apollo.
See you later." They wiggled their fingers at each other
as Artemis left. Once outside the arena, she squeezed
her eyes shut and tried chanting again:

"Come, my twin, give me a clue—
a picture I can use to find you!"

After a few seconds, a vision of a room swam into view. It was blurry, though, so Apollo must still be blocking her, Artemis thought. Likely he was concentrating so hard on something else that he'd half-forgotten to shut her out. Now was her chance to find him!

She squinted, trying to figure out what she was seeing. Long things . . . breadsticks? No . . . batons? No! *Textscrolls!* Lots and lots of textscrolls on shelves. The MOA library? It had to be. Maybe he'd gone there to study for the Revenge-ology quiz. To tell the truth, she should be doing the same, not chasing after her brother!

Nevertheless, Artemis raced back to the Academy to look for him. Bursting through MOA's front doors, she hurried up the hall and then downstairs to the library. "Apollo?" she called out as she entered.

Mr. Eratosthenes, the librarian, looked up. He was wearing some weird binocular-looking glasses, so she couldn't see his eyes. A mapscroll lay unfurled on the desk before him, and it appeared he'd been making notations on it. His lips moved like he was saying something, but she couldn't hear him. He was the quietest librarian—or person—she'd ever met.

Artemis glanced around the room, but except for Mr. Eratosthenes, the place was deserted. "Have you seen my brother, Apollo?" she asked.

Mr. Eratosthenes lifted a hand and focused his binoculars in her direction, as if to see her better. "Godboy? Taller than you, but same dark hair and eyes?"

His voice was too quiet to hear, but she'd read his lips this time. "Yes, that's him."

The librarian glanced around the room. "He's not here," he announced. At least that's what she thought he'd said. Either that or "Bee snot fear," and that made no sense. Refocusing the binoculars again, he went back to making notes on his mapscroll. Every time he wrote something, Artemis noticed that it caused the map to magically alter. Boundaries between lands shifted, seas grew or shrunk, and mountain ranges sprang up.

"Was he here earlier?" she persisted. Honestly, it was like pulling teeth to get anything out of this guy. Weren't librarians supposed to help kids seeking information?

"Possibly," he whispered, not looking up from his work. "Do you expect me to remember everyone who comes in and out of here?"

Ye gods, thought Artemis. The place was *empty.* Apparently Mr. Eratosthenes was so caught up in his mapscroll he couldn't pay attention to the comings and goings of even one single student!

Artemis took a quick tour around the library on her own, but Apollo was nowhere to be found. She was sure he'd been here, though—she'd seen this place in her vision!

The library shelves were stacked high, but the most valuable and rare scrolls in here were housed in storage cabinets, called armaria. When Artemis noticed a scroll sticking out of a half-open door on one armaria, she went closer. She peeked at the scroll's title: *The Caves of Parnassus.* Parnassus? Hmm. Why did that ring a bell?

Pulling out the scroll, she unrolled it atop the nearest table to take a look. Her eye was quickly caught by five fearsome words. "Cave of the Parnassus Python." Aha! Now she recalled why the name "Parnassus" sounded so familiar. It was where the infamous Python was from! So Apollo hadn't come here to study for their quiz at all. He'd been looking for information about the terrible serpent he planned to match wits with in the biggest, baddest event of the Olympic Games. The Python-o-thon!

Had he hoped to find out if the Python had any

weaknesses? If that had been his goal, this scroll didn't seem to offer any help. It described the serpent as a "frightful monster," mentioning that it lurked in the Parnassus Caves and "did dreadful things to thin-legged sheep and their owners as well."

Ye gods! Apollo didn't own any sheep, but his legs were kind of skinny. Her concern for him increased. Would Python make a meal of her brother if they tangled?

Python couldn't kill Apollo—he was immortal, after all—but what if it gulped him down whole? Her poor brother would have to remain in its stomach until it chose to barf him back up. And that would mortify him in front of his friends. It might take him ages to recover. Besides, who wanted to be barf, even for a few minutes!

Artemis rolled up the scroll and put it away, then

closed the armaria. Squeezing her eyes shut, she whispered their chant, trying to see where Apollo had gone. But no image came. And that could only mean one thing: Apollo was playing Keep Away.

So that's why the armaria had been left open, she realized. He'd felt her trying to "see" him and had left in a big hurry, figuring she was hot on his trail! Did he think she was going to take another stab at talking him out of entering the Python-o-thon? Or had he heard about the petition and didn't want to sign it? Whatever the reason, Artemis was through chasing after him. He wasn't the only one around here whose feelings could get hurt. If he didn't want to see her, then fine. She'd leave him alone. Let him see how well he got along without her!

When she got back to her room, her dogs practically bowled her over as she opened the door. At least *they* were happy to see her! She sat on the floor and gave them all a group hug, burying her face in their cool fur. For some reason, she sort of felt like crying. She hated fighting with Apollo. Luckily, being with animals had always had a soothing effect on her and she eventually calmed down.

While she was setting out fresh dog food and water, someone knocked on her door. Hope surged up in her. "Apollo?" she called out. Even though boys weren't supposed to visit the girls' floor, they sometimes did. Like when they had important apologies to make to their sisters.

"No. It's me," said Aphrodite through the door.

"Oh. Come in," said Artemis, hoping her disappointment didn't show.

Aphrodite opened the door an inch at a time, edging inside while keeping a sharp eye on the dogs. She didn't exactly *dislike* dogs, but she definitely wasn't as fond of them as Artemis's other friends. She didn't like anything the least bit messy. Thinking about that made Artemis smile inwardly. It was a wonder that Aphrodite liked *her*!

"Want to sit?" With a sweep of her arm, Artemis pushed the ratty chiton she slept in, plus a couple of arrows whose tips she'd been meaning to sharpen, and some other random junk, off her unmade bed and onto the floor.

Aphrodite's fingers twitched and Artemis had a feeling she was itching to clean up the mess. "Uh, no. Thanks anyway," Aphrodite replied. "I just have a sec. I'm meeting Ares downstairs. He wants me to time him in a practice run."

"So late?" Artemis asked in surprise, glancing toward the darkness outside her window. Of course, the track would be lit up with torchlights.

"I think that's the idea," said Aphrodite. "He'll have the whole track to himself. He said it's hard to practice with those giants shaking the ground with all their stomping."

"Is that what started yesterday's fight in the hall?"

Aphrodite shook her head. "No. According to Ares, Ephialtes stepped on the heel of his sandal and tripped him. Ephialtes said it was an accident, but Ares thinks otherwise." She sighed. "Putting two hotheaded guys together in one Olympics is a recipe for disaster. Especially if one is the god of war and the other is a bad-tempered giant. Anyway," she said, changing the subject, "I wanted to ask if you think we should set up tables in the courtyard again tomorrow morning."

"Definitely," said Artemis. "We got a lot of signatures today, but we could use more. We can take turns manning the tables all weekend. If you see Athena and

Persephone, tell them. Ditto, if I see them first."

"Deal," said Aphrodite, turning to go.

"Is that one of our petitions?" Artemis asked, noticing the pink scroll tucked under her arm. The other three were stashed in her quiver for safekeeping.

"Uh-huh." Aphrodite smiled mischievously. "Speaking of deals, I told Ares we could do one. I'd time his run if he'd sign our petition."

Artemis jerked her head back in surprise. "And he agreed?"

Aphrodite nodded.

"That's amazing! He'll be our first immortal boy to sign! And you only need to time his run?"

Aphrodite grinned. "Well, I also told him that if he *didn't* sign, I was going to buy Ephialtes a nectar shake at the post-Games celebration at the Supernatural Market."

"Ha! That would do it," said Artemis.

After Aphrodite left, Suez began to whine and scratch at the door, wanting to be let out. "All right," Artemis agreed. "But it's going to be a short walk." She slung her quiver over her shoulders and grabbed her bow. When she opened her door, all three dogs tore down the hall ahead of her and then leaped their way down the marble staircase.

Just as she caught up with them at the bottom of the stairs, Actaeon appeared. Instantly, her dogs mobbed him.

"Down, boys!" Artemis ordered. At her command, the dogs stopped jumping, but they still sniffed at him curiously. "Sorry," Artemis told him. "I don't know what's gotten into them."

Actaeon shrugged good-naturedly. "Maybe it's the lingering whiff of *eau de stag?*"

She felt her cheeks grow rosy with embarrassment. "I'm really sorry about that—turning you into a stag, I mean. I admit I overreacted."

"It's okay." Actaeon knelt to scratch Nectar behind the ears. Not one to miss an opportunity, Suez rolled onto his back, and Amby, wagging his tail, braced his front paws against Actaeon's leg and stretched his neck to look adoringly up at him. "It was actually an interesting experience," Actaeon said, somehow managing to pet all three dogs at once. "Have you ever been a stag?"

"Uh, no."

"Well, you wouldn't believe how heavy antlers are! And if I could run that fast all the time, I might actually have a chance at beating Ares in the footraces on Saturday."

Artemis laughed. But when Actaeon stood again, an uncomfortable silence fell.

"Well . . . ," she said, edging for the bronze exit doors.

"Wait." He stepped toward her. "I didn't mean to push you into the fountain yesterday. It was an accident. Someone shoved me. And it wasn't me that shouted, *'Protect me, Artemis,'* either."

"Good to know," she said, nodding. "I wondered."

"And I'm sorry I laughed."

"S'okay. I guess I did look funny."

"You could push *me* into a fountain if you want," Actaeon offered.

Artemis grinned. "Thanks, but I think turning you into a stag makes us even." She decided not to tell him that she'd been trying to pull him into the fountain when she fell in the second time. Her dogs ran over to the front doors, eager to get outside.

"Going for a walk?" Actaeon asked.

"Uh-huh."

"Want some company?"

"I won't be out long—just long enough for my dogs to go to the . . . well, you know." Her face warmed again. Why had she said *that*?

"Oh," said Actaeon, taking a step back. "Sure. Another time, then." He turned to go.

"I almost forgot," Artemis said. "Thanks for signing the petition."

"No problem," he said. "Hope it helps." He started up the marble staircase, quietly whistling her favorite Heavens Above song.

Godsamighty! Artemis thought as she watched him go. Why couldn't she have just said *yes* when he asked if she wanted some company? No wonder she was the only one of her friends without a crush. Not that she wanted one, of course. Still, Actaeon *was* kind of cute. And nice. And her dogs liked him.

She took her hounds outside and walked them around the edge of the courtyard. After they did their dog business, she quickly corralled them. "Longer walk tomorrow," she promised. As they reentered the Academy and climbed the stairs to the dorms again, she kept hoping she'd run into Actaeon. *What did you expect him to do? Sit on the stairs and wait for you?* she chided herself. Besides, she didn't really have anything to tell him. She just thought it might be, well, fun to hang out with him.

After leaving the dogs in her room, Artemis knocked on Athena's door, wanting to talk. She heard voices inside. Then Pandora, Athena's roommate, opened up. She was wearing blue pj's, decorated with a pattern of gold question marks. "Want to come in?" she asked. "I was just going down the hall to shower—uh-oh, did I forget my toothbrush?" Even when something didn't start out to be a question, Pandora could make it into one.

"Thanks," said Artemis. She stepped in, and Pandora stepped out.

Athena was sitting against the pillows on her bed with her knees drawn up. Her purple Revenge-ology textscroll rested on her lap, reminding Artemis that she still needed to study for the quiz. "Hey," Athena said, glancing up. "We all went to the Supernatural Market for shakes after the match." She set her Revenge-ology scroll aside and wrapped her arms around her knees. "Some of the guys said Apollo signed up for the Python-o-thon."

Artemis flopped down on Pandora's bed, which was opposite Athena's. "Yeah, he said he was going to." She picked up the glittery Magic Oracle Ball sitting on Pandora's bed. About the size of melons, these balls were made by fortune-tellers and sold in the Immortal Marketplace. "Is there a way my brother can beat the Python?" she asked it. Holding her breath she tossed the ball in the air. Both girls leaned in, eagerly awaiting its reply.

The ball spun crazily and then spoke its magic answer: "True and False."

"Excuse me? What's that supposed to mean?" said Artemis.

Athena laughed. "That's a typical oracle for you. Difficult to figure out."

Artemis caught the ball in her open palm again. "No kidding."

Athena took the ball from her and set it aside. "What I think is—Apollo must have a death wish to enter that contest. I'm glad Heracles didn't. He's mortal and I've heard Python can squeeze the life out of a body in less than—oh, sorry." She put a hand over her mouth as if she'd just realized she might be scaring Artemis. "Don't worry. Apollo is immortal. So he can't get hurt too badly."

"Not physically maybe. But the embarrassment of losing might kill him!"

"Then why chance it?"

Artemis stretched out. Resting her head in one hand, she looked over at Athena. "He's jealous of Heracles."

"Really?" Athena said with a look of surprise.

Artemis nodded. "You know how Heracles battled all those fierce, awesome creatures when you helped him perform his labors? And then to top it off, Zeus decorated his own temple with paintings of those labors? Well, that's the kind of glory and honor every godboy at MOA dreams of."

"But Apollo's a god!" Athena exclaimed. "Heracles

171

hasn't ever said so, but sometimes I can tell he longs to be one himself." She paused, then added, "What mortal doesn't?"

"Being a god isn't enough for my brother. He wants to win his own temple. Thinks it will earn him more *respect*."

"Respect?" Athena repeated. "Must be a boy thing."

Artemis nodded. "I worry about him."

"Of course you do," Athena said sympathetically. "It's only natural, since you two are so close."

Artemis looked away. "Not so much anymore. Lately everything I do seems wrong," she admitted, tracing a fingertip over the swirly design on Pandora's blue and gold bedspread. "If I try to help him, he gets embarrassed and mad. He thinks that sometimes I act like I'm his *mom*, instead of his sister!"

"Ouch!" said Athena.

"Yeah," said Artemis. "And when I tried to use our twin sense to find him tonight, he blocked me out."

"Probably thought you were going to ask him to sign our petition," Athena teased.

"I was," said Artemis, grinning at her. "Though I'm not even sure he knows about it yet."

Just then, a light tap sounded outside Athena's window. Both girls glanced up to see a rolled-up piece of papyrus hovering beyond the glass pane.

"Hold on," Athena called out as she crossed the room to open her window. As soon as she did, a gusty breeze pushed the scroll through the window, letting it drop to the floor.

One delivery done. Gotta run! the breeze murmured, rushing off.

Athena picked up the scroll, then squeaked and dropped it just as quickly. Tiny sparks fizzed from it, then fizzled out. "Uh-oh."

"From Principal Zeus?" Artemis went to look as Athena picked it up again, this time without mishap.

Athena nodded as she unrolled and skimmed the papyrus sheet. "And it's not good news." She let Artemis read the note:

DEAR THEENY,

I HEARD A RUMOR ABOUT YOUR PETITION
FOR A GIRLS-ONLY OLYMPICS. AS KING OF
THE GODS AND RULER OF THE HEAVENS,
I ORDER YOU TO STOP GATHERING
SIGNATURES. A PETITION WILL NOT

SWAY ME. THERE WILL BE NO GIRLS-ONLY

OLYMPICS. AND THAT IS FINAL!

YOUR LOVING DAD,

ZEUS

Artemis sucked in her breath. "Ye gods. What do we

do now?"

Athena sighed. "Not much we *can* do. My dad never

changes his mind once it's made up." She frowned.

"Who do you think told him about our petition?"

"Not Pheme," said Artemis. "She supported the

idea."

"One of the boys, then?" Athena asked.

Artemis nodded. "Probably." She just hoped it wasn't

Apollo. *She* hadn't told him about the petition, but plenty of other people might have.

No matter, though. It seemed that their girls-only Olympics idea was doomed before it even got off the ground. She didn't look forward to telling all the girls who had supported them. They were going to be as disappointed as she was!

11
Wedding Talk

I **HAVE NEWS THAT MIGHT CHEER EVERYONE**
up," Persephone announced at lunch on Friday.

"Good. We could use some," said Artemis. During
breakfast it had been all over the cafeteria that Zeus
had squashed the girls' hopes for their own Olympic
Games. As a result, there were a lot of unhappy girls.

Some of them, like Medusa, blamed Artemis for

having made them think a girls-only games was even possible.

"Hera is subbing for Ms. Nemesis again today," said Persephone, who had Revenge-ology first period. "Since the Games are tomorrow, and it's also the weekend . . ." She paused for dramatic effect. "Today's quiz has been postponed until Monday!"

Aphrodite let out a whoop. "Thank godness. At least something good happened!"

"Woo-hoo!" cheered Artemis. Her disappointment in the brakes being put on the girl-games had made it hard for her to concentrate on studying last night. And even though everyone else had given up, she was still spending a lot of time racking her brain for a way to change Principal Zeus's mind. So no way was she prepared for that test!

Only Athena, who had Revenge-ology right after

lunch, was unhappy about the news of the postpone-ment. "I don't see why we have to wait. Why couldn't Hera give the quiz?" she grumped.

Leave it to Athena to actually *welcome* a quiz, thought Artemis. But maybe if she'd studied for it as much as Athena probably had, she'd be upset too.

Later that afternoon when Artemis entered Revenge-ology, she immediately looked around for Apollo. He wasn't there yet. Ephialtes glowered at her as she passed him to go to her seat. "Heard about your dumb petition," he said in his funny, high-pitched voice. "Bet you won't get any boys to sign!"

He was obviously behind on the news, but she couldn't quite bring herself to be the one to inform him that Zeus had made the girls stop collecting sig-natures. Instead she heard herself say, "*Otus* did." As soon as the words left her mouth, she regretted them.

Ephialtes looked horrified. If she didn't want to make trouble for Otus, she'd better fess up about the petition getting the ax from Zeus. But before she could force the words out, Hera arrived and called for quiet.

"As most of you have probably heard by now, your quiz has been postponed until Monday," she announced. As everyone cheered, Artemis's eyes scanned the room. Still no Apollo. He never skipped. What was up? "Since I'm not an expert on revenge," Hera went on, "today I think we'll discuss something I do know about— marriage customs in various cultures."

The boys groaned, but the girls whispered excitedly among themselves. Aphrodite sat up a little straighter, looking intrigued. Personally, Artemis thought it was an off-the-wall subject to pick for Revenge-ology. Still, it was a subject Hera was an expert on, since she owned a bridal shop.

"I know this might seem an odd topic for this class," Hera continued, as if she'd read Artemis's mind. "However, I believe that anytime different cultures can reach a better understanding of one another, it can prevent misunderstandings and therefore defeat the need for revenge. Let's start with Greek customs," she said. "As you know, a Greek marriage ceremony begins after dark when the veiled bride travels in a chariot to the home of her groom."

Several girls sighed, thinking this romantic.

"Her family and friends walk beside her, carrying torches to light the way." Hera paused. "Who can add more?"

Pheme raised her hand. "There are musicians, right?" The words puffed from her lips in little cloud letters that lingered above her head. "Playing lyres and flutes."

Hera nodded.

"And along the way, other women throw flowers and fruits to the bride," said Aphrodite.

One of the boys in the back of the class made a muffled groaning sound and some other boys snickered.

"Hey," said Artemis, frowning over at them. "We do the same thing for athletes in a victory parade."

Hera smiled at her. "Yes, that's right. An interesting parallel, isn't it? What do you think about that? Is a wedding ceremony a woman's victory parade?"

Ares nodded. "Yeah, women win when they marry, and that means men lose big!" More hoots of agreement from the boys.

Aphrodite shot Ares a look. *He'd better be careful,* thought Artemis, *or his relationship with Aphrodite will soon be* off *again.*

"I'd rather seek victory in athletics than in marriage," Artemis insisted.

Before anyone could respond, Ephialtes spoke up. "We giants don't have a bunch of complicated customs. When we want to marry someone, we just carry her off."

The boys laughed, but the girls were indignant. "Without even asking her to marry you?" Aglaia protested.

"That's barbaric!" Aphrodite exclaimed.

"Demeaning and disrespectful too," added Artemis.

"Yeah," chorused the other girls. They glared at Ephialtes.

He hunched his giant shoulders. "I didn't make the rules," he muttered in a tiny voice. "That's just how we do it."

"Actually," said Hera, "there's a similar custom in

Sparta. After a man shows off his strength in a fight that's mainly for show, he tosses his bride over his shoulder and carries her off."

Artemis frowned. Whose side was Hera on? Ephialtes, of course, beamed at her.

"So what marriage customs do you think Principal Zeus would follow if he were to marry again?" Pheme asked slyly. Her words, embroidered with wispy wedding bells and pale doves, hung in the air for several seconds before fading.

Hera quirked an eyebrow at her. "I suppose that's a discussion for him and his bride-to-be."

The discussion continued on and class time flew by. When the end-of-the-day lyre bell sounded, Artemis and Aphrodite started toward the door together. "Zeus and Hera make such a cute couple," Aphrodite said. "I bet they get married."

Artemis recalled Hera's kiss on Zeus's cheek during the wrestling matches. "Yeah, it wouldn't surprise me." She glanced over at Hera, who was writing a note at Ms. Nemesis's desk. Making a sudden decision, she said, "I'll catch you later, okay? I need to talk to the teacher for a minute."

Without giving Aphrodite a chance to ask why, Artemis zoomed straight for Ms. Nemesis's desk. Seeing her, Hera looked up and smiled.

"Can I talk to you for a minute?"

"Of course, Artemis. What about?"

Shrugging off her quiver, Artemis dumped out the arrows, then stuck her hand down inside. "About this," she said, coming up with several crumpled sheets of papyrus. "They're petitions for a girls-only Olympics."

Taking the crumpled sheets, Hera smoothed them out on her desk and studied the signatures.

Artemis couldn't tell if she approved or disapproved. "It's not just my idea," she said quickly. "Athena, Aphrodite, and Persephone all helped. Lots of girls are interested. We even got a few boys to sign our petition. See?" She pointed to the boys on the list. Then she hesitated. "But Principal Zeus doesn't care. He says our petition won't sway him because his mind's already made up."

Hera's eyebrows rose. "Is that right?"

Excitement grew in Artemis as she sensed she was getting somewhere. Hera looked annoyed! "I was kind of hoping you could talk to him? I know he never changes his mind, but if *you* tell him a girls-only Olympics is a good idea, maybe he'll listen."

Hera sighed, tapping the petition with her pen. "I do think this idea is a good one. But Zeus and I have already—"

"And a *fair* one," Artemis interrupted.

"Tell you what," Hera said, gathering up the papyrus sheets, "let me keep these, and I'll see what I can do."

Score! thought Artemis. Maybe her idea wasn't doomed after all. "There's one thing, though," she had to add. "If Principal Zeus sees the signatures, I won't be getting the students who signed into trouble, will I?"

"No. I give you my word on that," Hera said solemnly.

As Artemis slung her quiver over one shoulder it occurred to her that before she'd cut Hera off she might have been about to say that she and Zeus had already discussed the idea of a girls-only games. That would explain the argument Artemis and Athena had witnessed at the wrestling match last night!

Artemis didn't want to cause *more* trouble for Hera, but then she seemed like a goddess who could stand up for herself. "Thanks," she said. "I—that is, we *girls*—really appreciate this."

Hera nodded. "I'll do my best." After a pause, she added, "But I can't promise I'll be successful. You know that, don't you?"

Artemis nodded back. "Whatever happens with Zeus, we'll all be thankful you tried." Her hopes were high as she exited the room, despite Hera's cautionary words. But she knew she'd better keep those hopes to herself. She didn't want to disappoint her friends and the other girls again. Hera was their last hope. If even *she* couldn't get Zeus to reconsider, their idea was truly D-E-A-D dead.

12

Python

AS ARTEMIS STARTED DOWN THE HALL, SHE saw a giant heading out MOA's front doors. Not sure if it was Ephialtes or Otus, she hurried after him. She had some explaining to do or there might be trouble.

Outside, she came to an abrupt stop. All over the courtyard below, groups of students were standing around, staring up at the sky. What were they looking at? Artemis didn't know, but she couldn't help looking up too.

High above them, Hermes' winged delivery chariot was disappearing into the clouds. It looked like he'd just taken off from MOA. Spotting Pheme a few steps below, Artemis hurried down to her. The goddessgirl of gossip was sure to know what was up!

The minute Pheme saw her, words puffed from her orange-glossed lips. "Hermes just dropped off the Python! I heard that it used its devious trickery on him and almost succeeded in gobbling him up in midflight." As cloud-words sailed above her head to form sentences, students nearby read them and gasped in alarm.

"Hmm," said Artemis. The first part of what Pheme said was probably true—that Python had arrived. As for the second part, well, Artemis was skeptical. Still, a shiver of fear for her brother's welfare skittered up her spine. Where was that boy anyway?

"The Python-o-thon is going to be so exciting!" Pheme exclaimed. "Too bad I'll have to miss the Games." She paused.

It took Artemis a minute to realize that Pheme was waiting for her to ask why she wouldn't be attending. "So, why do you have to miss?" she asked finally.

"Oh, it's nothing really," said Pheme. She paused again.

"If it's *nothing really*, then why don't you just get out of it?" Artemis asked as a feather drifted down to land at her feet. She figured it had come from the wings on Hermes' chariot.

"It's just a little ceremony I have to attend," Pheme

hastened to say as Artemis picked up the feather. "The people of Athens have decided to honor me with a small temple."

"Really?" Artemis stared at her in surprise. "What for?" She hoped her question didn't sound rude, but honestly, it seemed like temples were being handed out all over the place these days.

"It's in appreciation of all the work I did during Hero Week, arranging for girls to meet with Aphrodite," Pheme said proudly.

Artemis twirled the feather between her fingers. She'd been in Egypt at the time, but later, Aphrodite had told her about the matchmaking contest she'd held with Pheme's help in Athens.

Artemis was just about to congratulate Pheme when they heard someone ask, "Where's Python being kept?" Pheme dashed off to be the first to answer, "In the gymnasium! I saw Hermes' chariot take off from there just now."

That was probably true, thought Artemis. Since tomorrow's final event was to be held in the gym, housing Python there made sense. No one would want to move such a dangerous creature more often than necessary.

I'd really like to get a look at that serpent, she thought, tossing the feather away. Seeing it might give her some strategy ideas to pass on to Apollo! Of course, he'd made it crystal clear he didn't want her help—that he resented it, as a matter of fact. But he was her brother, for godness' sake. She *cared* about him. So Apollo could sue her in the Courts of Athens if he wanted—but she was going to try to help him anyway!

Before starting for the gym, she looked around for the giants. Spotting Otus and Ephialtes was easy. The two of them stuck out like enormous sore thumbs at the far side of the courtyard. From the tense looks on their faces, and all the excited gesturing going on, it appeared they were arguing. *Uh-oh.* Looked like she was too late to warn Otus about how she'd let slip that he'd signed the girls' petition. She hoped Ephialtes wouldn't be too hard on him about it!

She headed for the gym. As she reached the edge of the sports field closest to it, the ground began to shake. Turning, she saw Otus jogging downhill toward her and the fields.

Artemis intercepted him. "Was your brother mad about the petition?" she asked.

Otus sighed. "Yeah, he wasn't too happy I signed it."

"Sorry—I didn't mean to tell him. It just slipped out."

"Don't worry about it," Otus said with a shrug.

194

"Someone would've told him eventually. He'll get over it." He paused. "Ephialtes has a fierce temper, and we don't always think alike, but even so there's this bond between us that can't be broken." He peered into Artemis's eyes. "Know what I mean?"

She nodded, understanding completely. "It's like that between me and my brother too." *At least, it used to be*, she thought grimly. *She* still felt the bond—a combination of love and loyalty. But did Apollo?

A cheer went up as some runners zipped around the track nearby. "You're really nice, Artemis," said Otus. "A lot of students at MOA won't even talk to me. It's good to know I have at least one friend here."

"Hey, Otus!" Heracles called from the edge of the track. "Come over here, big guy!"

Artemis smiled. "Make that *two* friends."

Otus grinned at her, then waved to Heracles. "Be there in a sec!" He turned back to Artemis. "See you later?"

"Hope so," said Artemis. And she meant it. Especially now that she knew he only thought of her as the same kind of friend as Heracles. *Phew!* Good thing.

After he left, she continued past the track to the gym, trying to act casual. No one was around, so she tried the front door. Locked. A big sign on it read, Danger: Entrance Prohibited. A shiver ran down her spine. She knew she should leave, really she did!

But then she just happened to wander around the side of the gym by the loading and unloading entrances. *Might as well try the doors here,* she thought. *Just to see.* She reached out and tested them, each in turn. *Clunk!* One of them had been left unlocked! This was a dangerous situation. She'd better check it out. For the safety of everyone in the school!

At least that would be her story, if she got caught.

Creak! Artemis pushed open the door and slipped inside. She shivered as she found herself in a dark passageway. Pulling a silver arrow from her quiver, she blew along its length to make a torch to light her way. Slowly, the arrow began to glow. Her hands trembled slightly as she held the arrow-torch out in front of her and began walking. Without any kids around, this place was creepy.

One hall led to another, and soon the passage began to lighten. All too quickly, she came to an archway that led directly to the main gym, where the contest would take place tomorrow. Tiers of bleachers towered all around her, encircling the stage set in the center of the gym. Standing below it, she could see the monster. It was coiled up on the stage, like an enormous, scaly, pea-green cinnamon roll with yellow eyes.

Eyes? Artemis froze in her tracks, terror filling her. The Python was staring straight at her!

She began to back away. The serpent didn't budge. Why wasn't it reacting? Then she noticed it was making a weird sound—half hiss and half rumble. It was asleep! Of course—snakes didn't have eyelids and slept with their eyes wide open. She knew that from being around Medusa.

Edging closer again, Artemis fitted the notched end of her lighted arrow into her bow. She pulled the bow-string taut, resting the arrow tip on her non-shooting hand. With her bow at the ready, she felt safer as she slowly and carefully crept up the steps. Though it was scary to be doing this, it was also thrilling. She wasn't sure what she was here to learn. Something, though. Whatever might help Apollo when he came up against this beast!

The Python was leashed to a column at one side of

the stage, which had been covered with a bed of sawdust to make it comfy. The Esteemed Association of Beasts only accepted members who had fearsome talents of one kind or another. Even when invited to perform in an event such as the Olympics, these beasts had to agree to be tethered, lest they wreak havoc.

Still, Artemis had always had a soft spot for animals and knew they liked to roam free. Besides, all curled up, the Python didn't really look that dangerous. She couldn't help wondering if, had circumstances been different, she might've made it a pet. Like Medusa had made pets of the snakes that made up her snaky hair!

The serpent shifted in its sleep, sending a puff of sawdust in the air with a lazy swish of its tail. Suddenly, Artemis's nose twitched. She pressed the back of her wrist against it, trying to stop the sneeze she felt coming on. Uh-oh. *Aaaa-choooo!*

Her sneeze echoed throughout the gym. Immediately, the rumble-hiss sounds stopped. That big head whipped up. Python uncoiled in a flash. The tip of its tail lashed out, snatching Artemis up in the air in the blink of a cruel yellow eye.

"No! Put me down!" she yelled. Obviously this beast wasn't pet material after all!

"Or what? You'll ssshoot me?" Python hissed. It sounded amused. With a flick of its long, forked tongue it snatched the arrow-torch from her hands and hurled it away. "No, that would ruin tomorrow's contessst! And we don't want that, do we, my pretty?" It smiled, its sharp, fanged teeth gleaming in the dimness.

"Pretty? You must be mistaking me for my friend Aphrodite. If you let me go, I'll fetch her for you," Artemis lied, hoping to trick her way into release. She pushed at the coil around her waist, but it didn't budge.

What had she been thinking, coming here? Python was way scarier up close than she'd expected. Its mouth was so wide it could swallow her down in one big gulp!

"Certainly, I'll let you go," Python soothed wickedly, in a way that was not at all reassuring. "After you answer two quick quessstions."

"Questions?" Artemis stared into Python's crafty eyes. They were so mesmerizing . . . so hypnotizing. When they locked onto hers, she found herself unable to look away. Unable to struggle. Or resist.

"Quessstion number one," Python began, restlessly flicking its tail. "For what reassson are you here?"

Artemis panicked. She thought about making something up, but no sooner did the thought occur than Python warned, "I'll know if you lie."

"How?" asked Artemis, frightened, but also fascinated by this awesome serpent.

"You're right. I *am* rather awesssome, aren't I?" Python preened, its hard yellow eyes glittering and its monstrous mouth opening even wider in an eerie, threatening sort of smile.

Artemis gasped. "Are you . . . reading my *mind?*" Her voice rose in a squeak on her last word.

"Yesss, clever girl. As long as I hold your gazzze, I can indeed read your mind."

Artemis tried hard to close her eyes. She even tried to pinch her eyelids together with her fingers, but they wouldn't budge. She tried to turn her head, but it was no use. Her head was frozen in place, her eyes glued to Python's. "You've hypnotized me, haven't you?" she accused.

"Ah-ha-ha-ha-haaaa!" The serpent made a dry, rattling sound deep in its throat, and Artemis realized it was laughing. Or gloating. Whatever.

"I'll ask the quessstions. And you'd better ansssswer. Or elssse," it hissed. "Now, last chance to redeem yourself: For what reassson are you here?"

Against her will, Artemis heard herself speak. "I'm here to find out whatever I can about you so I can help my brother, Apollo, beat you in tomorrow's contest." Why had she said that? It was like this serpent was squeezing the truth out of her!

"Exxxcellent," Python hissed, writhing excitedly. "Now we are getting sssomewhere." Its forked tongue flicked in and out of its mouth like a whip. Artemis cringed away from it. Was she to be lashed to smithereens?

But Python only spoke again. "Time for quessstion number two: What isss your brother's greatessst weaknesss?"

Artemis clamped her hands over her mouth, trying

to avoid answering, but it didn't matter. The answer slipped into her mind anyway: *He cannot tell a lie.*

"Is that ssso? How very interesssting." The serpent stared hard at her, its body coiling and uncoiling restlessly, and Artemis knew it was searching her mind. What had she just done? Put poor Apollo in even more danger, that's what!

Evidently satisfied that she was telling the truth, Python laughed its dry, rattling laugh again. "Many thanksss," it said. Then the sly beast lowered her with surprising gentleness to the stage, unwound its tail from around her waist, and released her gaze. "You may go now! And let thisss visssit be our little sssecret, hmm?"

Shame washed over Artemis as she scrambled down the stage steps. Heart pounding, she grabbed her arrow-torch from where Python had tossed it as she ran through the arched entrance out into the passageway.

The serpent's raspy laugh followed her down the hall, echoing off the gym walls behind her. "Sssee you at the contessst!" it called.

Coming here had been a stupid mistake, she thought as she threw open the side door and raced outside. Whatever chances Apollo might have had at winning the contest, she was certain she'd just spoiled them. *Arghhh!*

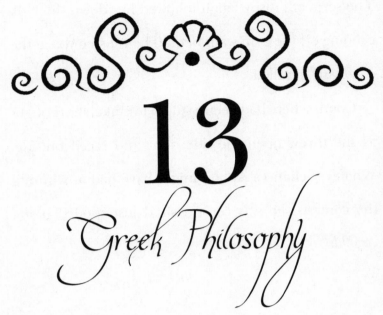

13
Greek Philosophy

APOLLO WAS GOING TO BE MEGA-ANGRY when he found out what she'd done. Still, Artemis knew she had to tell him. It would be dangerous for him to tangle with Python without knowing it was aware of his weakness. But where was he? She tried to find him using their twin sense, but he was still blocking her out, the blockhead!

So she had to search the hard way instead. She ran around looking high and low for him at the various Olympic practice trials that were underway. When she couldn't find him on the sports fields, she squeezed her eyes shut and tried one more time to get a fix on where he was. Finally, it worked! Which probably meant he was once again concentrating so hard on something that his attention had strayed and he'd forgotten to block her. A vision of a stone bench surrounded by olive trees floated into her mind. The olive grove! It was just beyond the school courtyard, and she made a beeline for it.

Sure enough, she found Apollo there, sitting on the bench, his nose so deep in a textscroll that he didn't even notice her at first. The title on the outside of his scroll read *Paradoxes of the Greek Philosopher Eubilides.* "So here you are," she said.

Startled, Apollo let go of the scroll and it rolled itself shut with a loud *snap!* The momentum sent it shooting off his lap to land on the ground a few feet away. "Whoa! Give me a heart attack, why don't you?" he said. But then he grinned at her as if everything was cool between them—as if he hadn't cut Revenge-ology to avoid her, though he most definitely had. She was glad he was in a better mood, but it wouldn't last. Not once she told him how she'd just destroyed any teeny chance he might have had at besting the serpent in the Python-o-thon.

Stalling for time, she motioned toward his textscroll as he went to pick it up. "What's a paradox?" She might've already known if she'd taken Philosoph-ology, but she hadn't had room for that in her schedule yet.

"It's kind of like a verbal puzzle. A statement that seems true, yet when you try to actually reason it out, it no longer makes sense." Retrieving the scroll, Apollo tossed it to the bench he'd just left and stuck his hands in the pockets of his tunic. "I guess you're wondering why I'm reading about them, huh?"

Artemis shrugged. "For class?"

He hesitated, as if he wanted to say "yes," but couldn't quite make himself. Which meant it wasn't for class. *Not being able to tell even little white lies must get old,* thought Artemis.

"If you must know," he said at last, sounding defensive, "I'm trying to further prepare myself to match wits with Python tomorrow."

"Oh. Yeah, about that," Artemis said, gulping. "There's something I need to tell you. And you're not going to like it."

He glowered at her. "If you're going to try to talk me out of entering the Python-o-thon again, then save your breath."

Artemis rolled her eyes. "Just listen, okay? And when I tell you, try to remember I'm your friend, *not* your enemy."

"Hey! You're scaring me now," Apollo said, sounding like he was only half-joking. "Out with it. I can take it."

She leaned against the trunk of an olive tree, one of many Athena had planted here to create this grove. Taking a deep breath, she let everything spill out. How she went to visit the serpent and was yanked off her feet. How Python's eyes had locked onto hers so that she couldn't look away.

"Godsamighty!" said Apollo, sounding worried for her. "That wily beast didn't hurt you, did it?"

"No."

"Good thing. You took a terrible risk going near it by yourself. I can't believe you did that." He ran a hand through his hair. "Well, at least you're okay."

"Mm-hmm," she said, pushing off the tree. "But there's one more thing. You see, when Python had me all hypnotized and at its mercy and everything, it asked me what your greatest weakness was."

"Don't tell me you told it?" demanded Apollo, spreading his arms in disbelief.

"No! Are you kidding? I wouldn't do that. But it found out anyway by reading my mind!"

Apollo frowned. "Ye gods! A mind-reading serpent! So what were you *thinking* my greatest weakness is?"

Artemis scuffed at the ground with the toe of her sandal, hoping that when she told him he wouldn't feel insulted. "That you cannot tell a lie." Hunching her shoulders, she braced for her brother's fury.

Instead of getting mad, though, Apollo only began pacing, looking like he was thinking hard. Finally, he stopped and turned to her. "Do you think Python believed you?"

Artemis nodded. "I told you. It read my mind. It *knew* I was telling the truth."

Then Apollo did the weirdest thing ever. He came over and gave her a hug! "Thanks, sis! You've just given me more help than you can possibly know."

"Wha . . . ?" Before she could ask him to explain, they heard footsteps. Actaeon burst into the grove, then abruptly halted. "Oh, hi," he said looking from one to the other.

"What's up?" asked Apollo. "You here to see me about something?"

"Actually," said Actaeon, the tips of his ears turning bright red, "I wanted to talk to Artemis."

"Well, go ahead. There she is," Apollo said, gesturing toward her. Artemis's cheeks felt warm. She was sure they must be as red as Actaeon's ears. And she was equally sure that Apollo had noticed. He was grinning now, in a teasing mood.

Actaeon shifted from one foot to the other as if he were trying to think up an excuse for having come. Looking at Artemis, he said, "I . . . um . . . heard your voice, and I . . . um . . . just wanted to say I was disappointed when I heard that Zeus won't let you keep on with your petition."

"What petition?" asked Apollo. He'd been in his own little world so much the past few days, he apparently hadn't heard!

"My friends and I were gathering signatures to try to convince Principal Zeus to let us start a girls-only Olympics," Artemis told him. "We got over sixty kids to sign our first day. Only then Zeus found out about our petition and made us stop."

Apollo rolled his eyes. "I wish I'd known. I could've told you it was a bad idea."

"Yeah, well, some boys didn't think so," Artemis said stiffly. "*Actaeon* signed!"

"What?" Apollo looked at him like he was some kind of traitor. "Why would you do that?"

"Because I'm on the side of fairness," Actaeon said, sweeping away a strand of light brown hair that had fallen in front of one eye. "Girls should have their own games if they want. Why not?"

Artemis felt herself falling a little more in like with this boy! "I haven't given up," she said, as much to Apollo as to Actaeon.

Her brother raised an eyebrow. "Please tell me you're not planning to disobey Principal Zeus!"

"No," she said. "But I—" She paused, not wanting to tell him about Hera and how she was the girls' last hope. After all, Hera had warned her that even *she* might not be able to get Zeus to take the girls-game idea seriously. "—I meant to say that I haven't given up *hope*. Maybe Zeus will change his mind."

Apollo snorted. "Fat chance."

"Well, at least you fought for what you believe in," Actaeon told her. "You tried to change things. I admire you for that."

"Really? Thanks," said Artemis. He was such a sweet boy. *And* cute. But not in a flashy way like Orion, her first crush. Sweet was way better than flashy, she decided.

Ahem. Apollo cleared his throat extra-loudly to get their attention. Artemis jumped, realizing she and Actaeon had both just been standing there, staring at each other. What was wrong with her? Sure she was goddess of the moon, but mooning over a boy wasn't like her at all!

"Just curious," said Apollo, "how many boys actually signed your petition?"

"I'm not sure," said Artemis. She didn't know if Hades and Heracles had actually had time to sign the petition before Zeus squashed the girls' ambitions.

"Ten?" Apollo guessed.

"Maybe not quite so many," Artemis admitted.

"More than five?"

"Um . . . at least three."

"And I'm proud I was the first," Actaeon put in.

Apollo looked unimpressed. Sitting on the bench again, he unrolled his scroll. "No offense, but I need a little peace and quiet. I've got some work to do before tomorrow's contest."

"Sure, no problem." Actaeon glanced at Artemis. "I'm going to head back to the dorms."

"I'll go with you," Artemis said quickly and Actaeon looked delighted.

"Later, then. You guys have fun!" Apollo flashed Artemis a grin.

Ignoring his teasing, she said, "Yeah. Whatever. Bye." His jabs about the petition aside, she was glad he didn't seem to dislike Actaeon the way he had Orion. She did care about Apollo's opinion even if he didn't care about hers—at least not where Python and the Her-O-Lympics were concerned.

As she and Actaeon walked back across the court-yard, she stumbled over an uneven tile that had been struck by one of Principal Zeus's thunderbolts during his bad mood pre-Hera era. Actaeon caught her arm and steadied her. "You okay?"

"Yeah." She smiled at him, and then he surprised

her by curling his hand around hers. Her eyes went wide, but she didn't pull away. Still, she was thinking hard about what he had done and why he'd done it. It definitely meant he liked her. She didn't need Aphrodite to figure that out! Hands linked, they started walking again.

Only when they reached the top of the Academy's granite steps did he drop her hand. He moved to open the bronze doors, but Artemis was quicker. "I'll get it!"

"Uh, thanks," he said, moving past her as she held the door open.

"You're welcome," she said. Then it dawned on her that *he'd* wanted to hold the door open for *her*. "You can get the next door," she told him.

He chuckled. "Sure thing." Chatting together easily, they took the staircase. At the entrance to the fourth-floor dorms Actaeon made a show of holding the door open for her as they separated. Artemis smiled at him and then practically floated down the hall to her room. She'd never felt so light before, not even with Orion. Actaeon had said he admired her for fighting for what she believed in and trying to change things. Wasn't that nice of him? She smiled to think how her opinion of him had reversed itself so completely. It was only two days ago that she'd turned him into a stag!

Although the next morning was Saturday, Artemis got up even earlier than she would have for school. It was Olympics Day! After dressing quickly, she took her dogs on a long walk before breakfast. They were going to have to stay in her room all day, so she wanted to tire them out. It would be too dangerous to take them to the Games. Although they couldn't get into much trouble playing Dodge-the-Student in the hallways, it would be a disaster if they dashed between the runners in the footraces or tried to catch a flying discus.

Later, when Artemis reached the arena, she saw it was festooned with colorful flags from all of the participating schools, including the blue and gold of MOA. Athena had arrived early and saved space for her friends on a bleacher only a few rows above the stage. It was a good thing, too, as the arena was now packed full.

"Pardon me, excuse me," Artemis said, trying to avoid stepping on toes as she made her way over to her friends. When she reached them, she squeezed in between Persephone and Aphrodite. The first event was to be the wrestling contest. The four goddessgirls buzzed excitedly about who they thought would win and receive the traditional honor of being crowned with an olive wreath. As in all the events, there would be prizes as well, including gift certificates to shops in the Immortal Marketplace and no homework for an entire month.

Ta-ta-ta-TAH! As the wrestlers entered the arena, three heralds each lifted a long narrow bronze tube with a bell on its far end to his lips and blew. The trumpetlike instrument was called a salpinx, and upon hearing its notes, the crowd quieted. In unison, the heralds then announced the schedule of the day's events.

Each seemed to be trying to shout louder than the others, as if the very act of making themselves heard was an Olympic event they were vying to win. And since each one was from a different school, that was quite possibly the case!

As the first pair of wrestlers began to grapple, Artemis spied Principal Zeus and Hera. They were sitting way down in front at stage level upon two blue and gold velvet thrones. Zeus was dressed in a blinding-white satin tunic with a sash of MOA's blue and gold, and when he moved his arms, his wide gold bracelets flashed in the sun. He looked every bit the King of the Gods today!

Hera looked regal too, wearing a shimmery blue chiton, belted at the waist with a delicate gold chain. Her thick blond hair had been wound into an elaborate knot, and jutting from it was a fan of iridescent peacock feathers.

After several elimination matches, the wrestling semifinals came down to just two pairs: Otus vs. Heracles, and Ephialtes vs. Atlas. There were lots of throws and thumps during their matches, but no one was pinned. Finally, Heracles was declared the winner of his match, and Ephialtes of his. Otus looked a little disappointed to have lost, but like the good sport he was, he shook

Heracles' hand and clapped him on the back. Now Heracles and Ephialtes would battle it out for the crown!

"Go Heracles! Woot woot!" shouted Artemis. She hadn't wanted to cheer too loudly for Heracles when he was matched with Otus, since Otus was her friend too. But now she cut loose! As Ephialtes and Heracles faced off for the final match, Artemis leaned past Aphrodite to speak to Athena. "Do you think Heracles can beat him?"

"I hope so," Athena replied, clasping her hands in her lap so tightly that her knuckles went white. "I think he cares more about winning this championship than he did about completing the twelve labors my dad assigned him." Since Heracles wouldn't have been able to stay at MOA if he hadn't completed those labors, that was saying a lot!

As Artemis leaned back in her seat again, Aphrodite put a hand over Athena's and squeezed briefly, lending support.

Standing face-to-face, Heracles and Ephialtes circled around each other. Suddenly the giant lunged. Locking his hands behind Heracles' lower back, Ephialtes pressed his forehead into Heracles' chest and pulled him forward, forcing the mortal boy to bend backward.

Athena sucked in her breath. "Ye gods. An *inverted bear hug!*"

The crowd, most of whom were rooting for Heracles, groaned.

"That's gotta hurt," said Persephone, wincing as Ephialtes forced Heracles lower and lower.

Athena clapped her hands over her eyes. "I can't watch! Tell me when it's over."

Just before Heracles' shoulders could touch the mat,

bringing him dangerously close to losing, he somehow managed to thrust Ephialtes away and spring free. The crowd roared its approval.

"You can look now," said Aphrodite. "He's fine."

Athena dropped her hands to her lap. "Phew. That was a close one."

"How do you know?" teased Artemis. "Were you peeking through your fingers?"

"Maybe a little," Athena admitted with a grin.

Heracles and Ephialtes were circling each other again. The goddessgirls whistled and cheered and waved homemade banners they'd made during the week, calling:

"Heracles–he's our man.

If he can't beat'em, no one can!"

Suddenly Ephialtes stumbled. Before he could regain his balance, Heracles grabbed him. He forced Ephialtes'

head down, locking the giant's own arm around it. Now Ephialtes was upside down with his feet in the air. It looked strange to see Heracles, a boy only about half as tall as the giant, holding him that way.

A group of onlookers in the stands cheered:

"Seize him, Squeeze him.

Her-a-CLES him!"

Athena's eyes sparkled with admiration. "That's called a *vertical suplex*," she said with awe. Now Heracles leaned over backward, using his own weight to slam Ephialtes onto his back. And there Heracles held him, triumphantly pinning the giant's shoulders to the mat, for a full three seconds—all it took to win!

As soon as Coach Triathlon signaled the end of the match, the crowd went crazy. Artemis spotted two girls she didn't recognize holding up a sign that read: I ♥ HERACLES. *Well, they can ♥ Heracles all they like,* Artemis thought, *but Heracles won't* ♥ *them back.* Athena had already captured his ♥.

Ephialtes still lay on the stage staring up at the sky as if he couldn't believe what had just happened. The heralds blew a fanfare on their salpinxes, then announced the official verdict in unison. "And the Olympic wrestling championship goes to . . . *Heracles!*"

The crowd went wild now, jumping up and down, and the goddessgirls joined in. "Bravo!" shouted Athena. "Bravo!" Artemis wasn't exactly sure if that was the right thing to shout at a wrestling match, but it didn't matter. Everyone else was yelling so loudly no one could really hear Athena.

Glancing back at the stage, Artemis saw that Ephialtes had finally gotten to his feet. As if frozen in place, he glared out at the crowd like they were some-how to blame for him losing the contest. Meanwhile,

Zeus rose from his throne and stepped onto the stage to congratulate Heracles and crown him with an olive wreath. Still, Ephialtes just stood there, scowling. *Why didn't he climb down from the stage and go sit on the bench with Otus?* Artemis wondered.

The heralds blew on their salpinxes again and announced that the footraces would be taking place next on the outdoor track. As was the custom at MOA, Zeus and Hera were first to leave the arena, followed by the teachers and coaches. The students had just risen to follow, when a yell came from the stage. "Hey! Stop! What are you doing?"

Artemis turned, just in time to see Ephialtes snatch the championship olive wreath from Heracles' head!

14

Stag Tag

GIVE ME THAT!" HERACLES DEMANDED. "I won it fair and square!" He tried to snatch the wreath back, but Ephialtes held it high, keeping it far above Heracles' reach. Then he dropped it on his own head.

"The championship should be mine!" Ephialtes shouted. "I deserve it!" He turned toward the crowd.

"You know I'm better than Heracles. I just stumbled is all."

Zeus and Hera and the other adults were long gone, but as soon as the students who had been pressing toward the exits heard the shouting, they turned back. When they saw what was happening, the MOA godboys rushed to Heracles' defense, jumping up on the stage to confront Ephialtes. In less time than it takes to shout "Godsamighty," a free-for-all broke out.

Several godboys jumped onto the giant's back reaching for the wreath, but he shook them off. More godboys grabbed on to his arms and legs. Otus leaped into the fray too, trying to protect his brother. Artemis was sure he wouldn't have approved of Ephialtes' wreath snatch, though. Otus and Heracles were friends after all, and it was obvious to everyone except Ephialtes that Heracles had won the championship.

As they wound their way down from the stands, Persephone exclaimed, "This has to stop before Principal Zeus finds out about it. He'll cancel the rest of the competitions!"

Cancel the Olympics? That would mean Apollo couldn't be creamed by Python! Artemis realized, looking on the bright side. On the other hand, although she might not think it fair that the Games were boys-only, she wouldn't want all those who had trained so hard to lose their chance to compete in the rest of the events. All because of Ephialtes' bad sportsmanship!

Athena's forehead furrowed. "Cancelling the competitions might not be the worst of it. This could lead to an Interworld catastrophe. It could even cause a war!"

War? You can't get much more catastrophic than that! thought Artemis. If only there was some way to get Ephialtes to leave the arena. The fighting would end for sure. Artemis thought hard. Suddenly she recalled Otus's words that day in Hero-ology: *"If there's one thing my brother can't resist, it's a hunt. He'd even abandon a pile of gold or, better than that, one of my mom's home-cooked meals to chase a stag."*

Artemis didn't need Ephialtes to abandon a pile of gold or a home-cooked meal, only a wreath! "I've got an idea how to stop this," she announced.

Aphrodite's brows rose. "What are you—"

But before she could even finish her question, Artemis had already begun chanting her spell:

"With my own hand, myself I tag.

Turn this goddessgirl into a stag!"

Squeezing her eyes shut, she visualized herself as a majestic stag with smooth brown fur and beautifully curved antlers. Instantly, she fell forward onto her hands and feet. Arms and legs became four sturdy limbs with hooves at each end. Her face grew longer and ant-lers grew from the top of her head. All around her, the audience and athletes shrieked, running to get out of her way.

In the next moment, she sprang from the stands. With a mighty leap, she was on the stage. As she had hoped, Ephialtes forgot all about the fight as soon as he saw her. The thrill of a hunt was too much to ignore and in a flash, he gave chase. As he thundered after her, a breeze whipped the wreath from his head. Before it hit the ground, someone caught it.

Artemis sailed over the stage and raced toward the exit. Turning her head briefly, she checked to be sure that Ephialtes was still behind her. He was. Otus was right behind him. Beyond them, she saw that the wreath had been tossed from student to student until it finally wound up in Athena's hands. Heracles bent toward her and she placed it gently atop his head. A cheer went up. The fight had ended!

But Artemis wanted to get Ephialtes far from the arena. If she didn't, he might go back and start something again. Once outside, she headed away from the sports fields. On strong, furred legs, she galloped down a trail that wound from Mount Olympus to Earth. Ephialtes followed, hot on her hooves. *Boom! Boom!* His footsteps pounded the earth, charging through the brush behind her.

As a stag, she could outrun any mortal or immortal. But Ephialtes was a *giant*. A really fast one! And Actaeon was right. Stag antlers were heavy! She could feel them weighing her down, and they kept getting snagged in the overhanging tree branches and vines. Stags had a lot to keep track of!

When Artemis reached a stream, Ephialtes slowed a

bit as he splashed into it. But she was able to leap across and gain some ground. She disappeared into a forest and zigzagged back and forth through the trees until she lost him. Her hope was that he'd give up and find his way home from here. When she came to a small glade, she stood there a while, panting.

Suddenly, Otus stepped from behind a tree at the far end of the glade. "Artemis?" he called out.

As she turned her antlered head toward him and bleated out a *yes*, a shout came from the other end of the glade. Ephialtes! He was charging toward her. "Run!" Otus yelled, speeding in her direction as if to protect her. Just as the two brothers raced up on opposite sides of her, she transformed herself into a hawk and flew away. Unable to stop quickly enough, the twins collided. Bumping heads, they crashed to the ground. *BOOM!*

Artemis swooped lower to land on a branch a safe

distance away, but close enough to eavesdrop. She wanted to make sure Ephialtes didn't plan to return to MOA. She also wanted to make sure Otus was okay.

"Ow," Ephialtes moaned in his girlish voice as he sat up. He pressed his hand to his forehead.

"You're bleeding," said Otus, pointing to a cut above his brother's left eyebrow.

"Well, you're missing a tooth," said Ephialtes, pointing to Otus's mouth.

"Where?" asked Otus, sitting up as well.

"Bottom row." Suddenly Ephialtes began to laugh.

Otus stared at him. "What's so funny?"

"We're identical again!" Ephialtes whooped. A slow grin spread across Otus's face as he realized it was true.

Laughing hysterically, they began to roll around amid the leaves like giant kids. Eventually, their giggles died away.

Lying on his back amid the leaves, Ephialtes sighed. "You know what I want?" Artemis crossed her talons, hoping it wasn't to go back to MOA to steal Heracles' olive wreath again. "A real meal for a change," the giant went on. "The Mount Olympus cafeteria serves such tiny portions. Even though I ate six trays of food at every meal, I'm starving all the time. It's no wonder I stumbled in that match. I was weak from hunger."

"That had to be the reason," Otus agreed. "If we head home now, Mom'll probably have dinner on the table by the time we get there. A humongous plate of her skunk cabbage stew, and you'll be good as new."

Ephialtes looked undecided, but Otus jumped up. "Last one there is a rotten giant!" he challenged. When he took off through the forest, Ephialtes couldn't resist leaping up to follow.

As the two brothers loped homeward, Artemis

circled overhead and let out a loud *cak-cak-cak*. Otus glanced up. When his eyes met hers, he nodded his approval, then winked.

Why, he'd challenged his brother on purpose—to get him to return home! Artemis realized. Curving her beak into a smile as best she could, she winked back. Then, as he waved good-bye, she tipped her wings and fluttered them in farewell. It made her feel a little sad to see him leave so suddenly. She promised herself that she'd write to him later to fill him in on the results of the rest of the Games.

As she flew back to the sports fields, Artemis thought about how different twins could be. Otus was as kind and big-hearted as Ephialtes was hot-tempered and reckless. Nevertheless, they were still brothers. And they were buddies. Just as she and Apollo had once been. And she wished so much they could be again!

The fields were deserted as she approached them. The footraces and other outdoor events must have already ended. That meant—oh no! The Python-o-thon! Heart pounding, she glided down to the gymnasium and took her goddess form again. Then she yanked open the gym door, dashed inside and down a hall to reach the main part of the gym.

It was so crowded that the audience had overflowed into the aisles. Artemis could hardly see the stage. As she elbowed her way through the crowd, she heard a boy cry, "Stop! I beg you. I can't take this anymore!"

Her heart plummeted until she realized the voice wasn't Apollo's, but some other unlucky boy's. When she finally made it close to the stage, she saw a mortal boy tightly wrapped in Python's coils. Since she didn't recognize him, she guessed he wasn't from MOA. In accordance with the contest rules, which forbade intentional physical harm, Python relaxed its hold on its victim, but didn't let him go. Twirling the tip of its tail like a lasso, the serpent grinned. "Yee-hah! Answer my question, or I'll make mincssemeat out of you, mortal!"

The crowd around her groaned. *"Boo! Hiss!"* someone yelled.

Python's cruel eyes gleamed. *"Hisss?* Now you're ssspeaking *my* language!" That familiar dry rattle of a laugh echoed through the gym. "Give up?" it goaded the boy.

Trapped in Python's coils, the boy could barely nod. "Say *theos*, then," prompted Python. Theos was the Greek word for uncle.

"Theos!" the boy cried.

Laughing wickedly, Python released him, its tail immediately sweeping him off toward the exit. "Begone, you fool. And count yourssself lucky. Many who match witsss with me don't live to tell the tale!" The boy coughed and sputtered as he reeled dizzily off the stage.

Lifting its head high, the Python swayed side to side. "Isss that the bessst you've got?" it taunted the audience. Its beady eyes scanned the gym as if searching for another challenger. "Don't be shy. Whoever's nexsst, ssstep on up!"

Artemis shuddered.

Ta-ta-ta-TAH! the heralds trumpeted on their salpinxes. "And now," they announced in unison, "fresh from his wrestling championship, we have our next contestant . . . *Heracles!*"

Heracles? Artemis jerked her head back. What was he doing here? Athena had said he wasn't going to compete! Judging from the surprised burst of chatter spreading through the crowd, no one else had expected him to either.

Artemis watched him confidently climb the steps to the stage. If Heracles beat Python before Apollo even got a chance to try, Apollo might be disappointed. But *she* sure wouldn't be!

Apollo liked Heracles, even if he was a little jealous of him. On the other hand, Apollo wouldn't exactly be happy if Heracles lost.

She surveyed the crowd, searching for her brother but not finding him. Instead, her eyes lit on Athena. She was determinedly pushing her way closer to the stage, with Persephone and Aphrodite right behind her. From the grim look on her face, Artemis knew that this had come as a complete surprise to her, too. She must be so scared for her crush!

15
The Contessst

"O VER HERE!" ARTEMIS YELLED TO HER FRIENDS.
She jumped up and down until they saw her and
veered in her direction.

The three goddessgirls looked relieved to see her
alive and well, but didn't ask about what had happened with the giants right away. They had other

more immediate concerns. "I don't know why Heracles is doing this!" Athena wailed.

"Maybe your dad put him up to it when he crowned him earlier?" suggested Persephone. They all glanced over at the principal. He and Hera were sitting front row center on their blue and gold thrones, which had been moved for them between each event.

As the girls watched, Zeus grinned at Heracles encouragingly, and even sent him a thumbs-up. From Zeus's relaxed attitude, Artemis doubted that anyone had told him about the fight in the arena after the wrestling match. It was a lucky thing Pheme hadn't been able to come to the Games!

"I bet you're right," said Aphrodite. "Zeus probably figured a contest between the Olympic wrestling champ and Python would be a spectacle worth watching."

That makes sense, thought Artemis. And though no

one said it, that must also mean Zeus didn't have much faith in Apollo's chances of beating the crafty serpent or even providing much of a challenge. *Ouch!* But she could understand such reasoning. After all, Heracles had proved his mettle against any number of beasts during his twelve labors. He'd have the best chance at winning of anyone!

Persephone put her arm around Athena and gave her a quick hug, to help calm her friend's nerves. Up onstage, Heracles approached Python now, his favorite trusty club braced against one shoulder, his championship olive wreath still perched on his head. Python eyed the club, then whipped its gaze toward Principal Zeus. "Contessst rules ssstate no weaponsss allowed."

Zeus nodded. "Sorry, Heracles," he boomed in a commanding tone. "Python's right!" As usual, his voice was so loud that the entire gym could hear him.

As Heracles reluctantly tossed his club to the far edge of the stage, Aphrodite whispered to Artemis. "You okay? We looked for you after we got outside. What happened to the giants?"

"I'll explain later," Artemis whispered back. She was just glad her effort to break up the fight had been a success. "Who won the other contests?"

Aphrodite beamed. "Ares won all three footraces."

"Awesome," said Artemis. "How about the rest?"

Persephone overheard and replied, "Hades won the long jump. He said it was because of all the practice he gets jumping over rivers of red-hot lava in the Underworld."

"And Hyacinth, a mortal from Earth, won the discus-throwing contest," said Aphrodite.

"Zeus should be happy," said Artemis. "Three of the four champions are from MOA!"

"And there's still this contest with Python," added Aphrodite. All four goddessgirls looked up at the stage.

Artemis could see that the serpent had already managed to lock eyes with Heracles. They were circling each other warily. "Yesss," said Python. "You're thinking that physssically you could beat me. However, thisss match will be about witsss."

From the look on Heracles' face, Artemis knew he'd just now figured out that Python could read his mind. Suddenly, he lost his confident bearing and began to look a tad nervous.

"I'll now pose two quessstions. When you fail to anssswer correctly—as you no doubt will—you'll cry *theos* and I'll win! I do ssso love to win!" Python hissed and snorted a few times. It was laughing at Heracles! All part of its master plan to demoralize him, no doubt.

"Bring it on!" said Heracles, his confidence seeming to return.

"Quessstion number one!" hissed Python, officially beginning their match of wits. "What creature movesss on four legsss in the morning, on two in the afternoon, and upon three in the evening. Yet the more legsss it gets, the weaker it becomes?"

Athena clenched her hands into fists. She leaned forward as if willing Heracles to figure out the answer.

Artemis wasn't very good at riddles, but it was a sure bet that Athena was. If only Heracles could read her friend's mind!

"Ha!" Heracles replied. "Easy peasy, Python. Because I've heard this riddle before. You stole it from the Sphinx who guards the entrance to Thebes."

Hearing this, Athena relaxed and even smiled. "Thank godness he knows this one!"

"The answer is humankind," Heracles said in a cocky voice. "Mortals crawl on all fours as babies, then walk on two feet as adults, and sometimes walk with canes in old age—as if the cane is a third leg."

"Well, I still don't get it," Aphrodite whispered to the other goddessgirls.

"Morning is early and symbolizes the first part of life—being a baby," Athena explained.

"Oh!" said Aphrodite, quickly catching on. "And afternoon is in the middle of a day, sort of like the middle of a person's life when they are an adult. And then evening symbolizes the last part of the day or the last part of life!"

"Very good, Heraclesss" said Python, pulling their

attention back to the contest. The serpent dipped its head and flicked its long, forked tongue. Artemis could tell it was being very careful to keep a distance between itself and Heracles. It was afraid of him! Interesting!

"Let's see how you fare with quessstion number two," Python continued. "A ten-year-old boy visitss the marketplace with two men—one thirty years old and one fifty years old. Without repeating any relationship—grandfather, father, or son, for example—can you name the five family relationshipsss between them?"

The crowd fell silent, and Artemis guessed that, like her, they were all trying to work out the answer to Python's question. It didn't seem like it should be very hard. The boy was probably the *son* of the thirty-year-old man, who was therefore the boy's *father*. And the fifty-year-old man would be the boy's *grandfather*. *That's three relationships,* she thought, counting on her fingers. Oh yes, and the boy would also be the *grandson* of the fifty-year-old man. So that made four. But what was the fifth? Then she remembered that the thirty-year-old man was the *son* of the fifty-year-old one. But that would make *two* sons and Python had said no relationships could be repeated.

Heracles must have been thinking along the same lines because he said, "It doesn't work for the boy to be the *son* of the thirty-year-old man. Hmm." Then he snapped his fingers. "I've got it! The boy isn't his *son* at all. He's his *nephew!*"

Python's tail went wild, slapping the stage, then whipping angry circles in the air. It was obviously worried Heracles had figured this one out, too, but it wasn't giving up yet. "Do go on."

"No problem!" Heracles grinned. "The fifty-year-old man is the *grandfather* of the boy, which makes the boy his *grandson*. So far, that's three relationships, including the nephew one. And the thirty-year-old man is the fifty-year-old's *son*. That's four. And since the boy is the nephew of the thirty-year-old man, that means the thirty-year-old man is his *uncle!*"

"Hisss what?" asked Python as if it hadn't heard.

"His uncle, his *theos!*" Heracles exclaimed.

Python grinned so widely then it bared its fangs. The whole audience gasped, fearing for Heracles' safety.

"Oh, no!" said Athena from beside Artemis. As usual she'd grasped what had happened a split second before everyone else.

"Yahoo! I win! I win!" Python rasped jubilantly. Stretching straight up in the air, the serpent twirled around on the tip of its tail. There was a moment of confusion before Heracles and everyone else caught on. Then they all let out a huge groan. The riddle had been a trick! Without meaning to, Heracles had cried "uncle" by uttering the word *"theos,"* which of course meant, "I give up."

"Poor Heracles," Persephone murmured. "He guessed both riddles, but he still lost!"

Heracles' shoulders slumped as he retrieved his club. He dragged it behind him and it bumped down the steps as he left the stage in defeat. Artemis glanced over at Zeus. He shrugged at Heracles and gave him a thumbs-up as if to say: *Oh, well. Can't win them all. Good job, anyway.* Zeus was a lot of things, but a poor sport wasn't one of them. Unlike Ephialtes.

The heralds blew on their salpinxes, quieting the audience. "And now for our last contestant!" they shouted. "Competing in his one and only Olympic event—give it up for Mount Olympus Academy's *Apollo!*"

Though Principal Zeus and the crowd cheered

253

politely, Artemis couldn't help cringing. Had it really been necessary for the heralds to mention that this was Apollo's *one and only* event?

As Apollo climbed the steps to the stage, Artemis whistled and clapped, showing her support. His hands were trembling, she couldn't help noticing. "C'mon, c'mon, you can do it, bro," she murmured to herself.

"Ssso," hissed Python, as Apollo approached. "We meet at lassst!" It made the dry, rattling-snorting sound that meant it was laughing. "I hope you're asss much fun as your sissster." Its face swung around to scan the crowd and Artemis instinctively ducked. No way was she going to let that sneaky snake hypnotize her into revealing any more secrets!

Aphrodite was staring at her in surprise, probably wondering where all of her supposed bravery had suddenly gone to. Peeking over the edge of the stage,

Artemis saw that the serpent had swung back to study Apollo. "Well, I certainly hope she's here watching because I wouldn't want her to misss your crushing defeat! Especially since it'll be partly her fault!"

Now *all* of Artemis's friends were staring at her. "What does it mean by that?" Athena asked.

Artemis gulped. "Tell you later," she promised, adding her earlier visit to see Python to the mental checklist of things she'd have to explain to her friends when all this was over.

Quick as a whip, Python coiled its tail around Apollo's knees and yanked him close. Its face lowered to within inches of Apollo's. Its yellow eyes glowed, seeming to will him to return its piercing stare.

But no matter how long and hard Python gazed at him, Apollo stubbornly kept his head turned aside. The serpent's head darted this way and that, trying to catch his eye. "What's wrong—scared to look at me?" it taunted, sounding frustrated.

"No, I just don't want you reading my mind," Apollo answered truthfully. After all, he couldn't lie.

"What's your second question?" Apollo demanded.

Python's head reared back in angry surprise. The goddessgirls' eyes all went wide and they looked at one another excitedly, realizing what Apollo had just done. He'd tricked Python into asking an easy question!

Watching Apollo stand up to Python, a newfound respect for her brother blossomed in Artemis. She realized he had every right to choose which battles he would fight, and that she couldn't—and shouldn't—try to fight all his battles for him. She'd thought she was being loyal, but maybe she'd just been bossy. And overprotective. No matter what the outcome of this contest, she vowed to try to respect his choices more in the future.

Unfortunately for her brother, however, Python seemed determined not to let him get away with the same trick a second time. "Oh, you're a clever one!" Python told him, sarcasm dripping from every word. "But no matter. I don't need to read your mind. Thanks to your sssister, I know your weaknesss. You're the boy who cannot tell a lie."

Still keeping his head turned away, Apollo said, "Then maybe you should think about this before you ask your next question: What I am saying now is a lie."

Distracted by this strange statement, Python's eyes narrowed and its tongue flicked in and out as the serpent thought hard. "That does not make senssse!" it hissed, shaking its head as if to clear it. "If what you just sssaid is true, and I know you to be the Godboy of Truth, then you were lying, even though your ssstatement wasss true." Releasing its tail from around Apollo's knees,

Python thrashed to and fro in a show of confusion. "But if your wordsss were a lie, then you were not actually lying, even though your ssstatement wasss a lie."

Thoroughly agitated now, the serpent began to twist its tail over and under its coils, tying itself into one knot and then another. Soon its head was swaying dizzily, and its coils resembled a very complicated yellow-green pretzel. "Thusss," it said at last, "if you were lying, you were telling the truth, and if you were telling the truth, you were lying!"

It was a *paradox*, Artemis realized, remembering the textscroll Apollo had been reading yesterday in the olive grove. Her brother had managed to present Python with a logic-confounding statement that was neither true nor false, and was therefore impossible to reason out! Suddenly she remembered the Magic Oracle Ball's answer when she'd asked if there was a way for Apollo to beat

Python. *True and false.* Now the ball's answer made sense!

Apollo grinned at the serpent. "Looks like I've got you tied up in knots. Give up?"

"Who, me?" asked Python. Then, realizing it had asked its second question by accident, it heaved a wild, frustrated roar. *"THEOSSS!"* The sharp-hissed admission of defeat echoed throughout the gymnasium. Then the serpent unkinked itself and slithered off behind the stage curtain.

Joy welled up in Artemis and she began cheering. But the stunned audience remained dead silent for at least three seconds. They were probably still trying to figure out Apollo's paradoxical statement! Finally, as Apollo turned to face the crowd, more cheers erupted. Raising both arms he flashed two *V*s for Victory. "I did it!" he yelled as if he could hardly believe it himself.

Then his eyes searched out Artemis's and they smiled

at each other. She flashed him the *V* sign in return.

BOOM! Zeus went from his throne to the stage in one leap. He was that excited! Placing an olive wreath on top of Apollo's head, he officially pronounced him the winner. "In Apollo's honor, a fabulous temple will be built in Parnassus! And now let's give a round of applause for *all* the contestants and all the champions in this year's Olympic Games," Principal Zeus thundered.

At this, applause and shouts shook the gym. When they eventually died down, he added, "Before you go, I have one more announcement—well, *two*, really—to make." The crowd went quiet as he summoned Hera to join him on the stage. Still dressed in her beautiful blue chiton, and with peacock feathers sprouting from her lovely hair, she looked both regal and dignified as she glided up the steps and went to stand beside him.

Artemis glanced at Athena. Her lips were pressed

together and she looked to be bursting with excitement. "You know what the announcements are going to be, don't you?" Artemis whispered to her.

Athena was beaming. "I know *one* of them." They both turned toward the stage just in time to hear Zeus say: "The first announcement is that Hera and I are engaged to be married!"

He paused for a minute while the girls all sighed and clapped in excitement. The boys soon joined in, cheering and whistling. "That's the one I knew about," Athena whispered.

"And now for the second announcement," thundered Zeus. He glanced at Hera fondly. "Before this lovely lady would consent to marry me," he said, "she exacted a promise that will make at least half of the students here very happy." He paused. "Soon there will be a new competition. One for *girl* athletes only."

At this, Artemis gasped. When she caught Hera's eye, Hera actually *winked* at her. Her talk with Zeus had worked! All of the girls in the audience—and to be fair, most of the boys, too—broke out in more applause. Apollo's win had put them all in a good mood.

"The new competition will be called the *Heraean Games!*" Zeus went on. "I came up with that—named it after Hera. Awesome idea, right?"

Artemis turned to her friends. "Hera bargained for the girls-only games for *us*! Isn't she the greatest?"

"Yes, and *so* fashionable," Aphrodite said, studying Hera admiringly. "I love the peacock feathers in her hair." Artemis had a feeling Aphrodite would soon be wearing feathers as well.

Athena glanced at Artemis anxiously. "You don't mind that Zeus changed the name of our games, do you?"

"Nuh-uh. Her-O-Lympics kind of stunk anyway,"

Artemis admitted. "And Zeus could've changed the name to chopped liver and I still would've been thrilled. We got our games! Woo-hoo! Can you believe it?"

The four goddessgirls did a group hug, hopping around in excitement.

Aphrodite beamed. "I can't wait for the wedding!"

"Do you suppose they'll need help with the flowers?" Persephone asked.

Athena laughed. "Ye gods! They only just got engaged!"

"I want to go congratulate Apollo," Artemis said, pulling away from the group hug as students began leaving the gymnasium.

"Don't forget about the post-Games celebration at the Supernatural Market," Athena reminded her.

"I won't. See you there!" said Artemis. With a quick wave, she was off.

Naturally, lots of students were eager to congratulate her brother. A crowd already swarmed around him onstage. Artemis hung back, waiting her turn. Seeing Hera behind her, she turned and said, "Thanks for what you did for us—for *all* the girls at MOA."

Hera's eyes twinkled. "Apollo's the one you should thank."

"Huh?"

The confusion in her eyes must've been plain because Hera said, "Oh, dear. I forgot I wasn't supposed to tell you. It's just the excitement of the engagement, I imagine."

"Tell me what?" asked Artemis, feeling even more confused.

Hera clasped her hands together. "After dinner last night I was in Zeus's office showing him your petitions when Apollo walked in. He handed Zeus some new pages to add to them. I don't know how he did it, but your brother managed to collect the signatures of every single boy in the MOA dorm."

She smiled at Artemis's gasp. "It's true that I told Zeus I wouldn't consent to marry him unless he approved the new games," Hera went on, "but that was *after* he saw all the names your brother had collected. I think that's what really changed his mind!"

Artemis's eyes glistened. "Apollo did that for me? For the girls?"

Hera nodded. "He told Zeus he really hoped the games would be approved. Not only because they were important to you, but because it was the fair thing to do." Hera paused. "You're lucky to have such a loyal brother."

"Yeah, but I wonder why didn't he want me to know?"

An amused smile played at Hera's lips. "If I recall correctly, his exact words were these: *'If she finds out I tried to help her, I'll never hear the end of it.'*"

"That sounds like something my brother might say," said Artemis, rolling her eyes.

Just then Principal Zeus came up to them. "Ready to go, my dear?" he said to Hera, offering his muscley arm. "Yes, my love," she replied, looking radiantly happy. After saying good-bye to Artemis, she took Zeus's arm. The two of them moved away looking like royalty, which they pretty much were.

The throng around Apollo had lessened some, so Artemis scooted closer. Up ahead, she saw Heracles clap Apollo on the back. "Congratulations, buddy," Heracles said heartily. "You were awesome. I wish I had your smarts!"

"Aw, don't be so hard on yourself," Apollo said.

"Python played a dirty trick on you. If it had tried that on me, I would've fallen for it too."

Heracles grinned. "Think ssso?" he said imitating the Python. They both laughed.

Apollo spotted Artemis just then. Carrying on with the joke, he addressed the admirers still in line, "Thanks for your congratulationsss, everyone. Gotta sssee my sssister now." He pushed his way over to Artemis. "Thanks, sis," he said, smiling broadly. "I couldn't have won without your . . ." He hesitated.

"Go on, say it! I already know," said Artemis, elbowing him in the ribs.

"Without your *help!*" He groaned, smiling. "I'm never going to hear the end of this, am I?"

"Nope!" said Artemis. She was just about to thank him for the boost he'd given the girl-games by talking to Zeus, when Medusa rushed over.

"You did it!" she shouted to Artemis, actually looking halfway happy for a change. "We got a girls-only games. Yippee!" She did a little dance.

Apollo and Artemis stared at her. Seeing her smile was so unusual that they were momentarily stunned. But dancing? That was just plain weird, especially for her.

Noticing their expressions, Medusa stopped in midjig, looking embarrassed. Flicking her snakes over one shoulder and acting cool again, she said, "At least they won't be named the Her-O-Lympics. What a lame-o idea that was!" Then she sauntered off, back to her normal sour self.

"Who cares what it's called!" said Artemis when she'd gone. "We got the games!" She imitated Medusa's happy dance and they both laughed. "Want to go celebrate with everyone?" she asked.

"Yes! Because I've got a lot to celebrate! Woo-hoo!" Apollo punched a victorious fist in the air. In the distance, other students looked over and cheered with him.

This was his moment, Artemis decided. Later, she would tell him what happened with the giants, and that she knew about the help he'd given her. Her eyes grew misty as she thought about it. But for now she just wanted to enjoy his happiness in beating Python and her own joy in the newly minted Heraean Games.

As they exited the gym and began walking toward the Supernatural Market, Apollo talked excitedly about the temple he'd won. "I know it won't be as grand as Zeus's newest temple, but mine will have a really good oracle."

"Mortals will *love* that," Artemis said. "And since you're the godboy of truth and prophesy, I bet they'll flock to your temple so they can learn what the future holds."

Squinting his eyes as if in deep thought, Apollo pressed two fingers against his forehead. "Yes, I can see that in my future. And I can see a temple in your future too—a *humongous* one."

"Really? Or are you just being nice?"

"I can't believe you asked me that!" he said, taking his fingers away from his head.

"Oh! Right. You can't lie! Wow, my own temple," Artemis mused, hardly able to believe it. Just imagine, mortals would go there to worship her. The thought would take some getting used to. Of course, she didn't know just when it would be built. Still, maybe it wasn't too early to start planning the decorations with her friends!

Just then they passed Actaeon, who was walking with Hades and Persephone. Actaeon waved and her heart gave a flutter as she realized he was heading for the Supernatural Market too. "Save me a seat!" he called to her.

"Okay, I will!" she called back.

"Ow, I got a rock in my sandal," said Apollo, stopping to shake it out.

Artemis barely heard him. She was too busy imagining Actaeon sitting beside her at a table in the Market. What would they talk about? Maybe they could compare notes about their experiences as stags! He might laugh at what she'd done, but this time, it would be in a good way. And while they were drinking their shakes, maybe her hand would brush up against his . . . accidentally, of course.

She was jolted back to the present when Apollo started to walk again. As she skipped ahead a few steps to catch up, Apollo squeezed his eyes shut and pressed his fingers to his head again. "Your temple will be built in Ephesus," he continued, as if prophesying. "And it is destined to become one of the Seven Wonders of the Ancient World."

Artemis gave him a thumbs-up, though she was sure he was overdoing it. "Wowza! Sounds good," she said to humor him. "But for now I'll settle for an ambrosia shake. Your treat."

Apollo smiled. "Race you there. Now that you've got your own girl-games, you're going to need lots of practice!" He took off, but Artemis soon caught up to him. Matching him stride for stride, she flew as swift as her fastest arrow, all the way to the Market.

READ ON FOR THE NEXT ADVENTURE

WITH THE

Goddess Girls

MEDUSA
THE MEAN

F ROM HER SEAT HIGH AT THE BACK OF THE
stone bleachers in the outdoor amphitheater at Mount
Olympus Academy, Medusa stared in fascination at
a full-page ad in her new *Teen Scrollazine*. It showed
a picture of a sparkly necklace with a golden-winged
white horse charm dangling from its chain. Her eyes
eagerly devoured the sales pitch:

At the bottom of the page was an order form.

Becoming immortal had been her dearest wish since, well, since forever. It wasn't fair that her two sisters were immortal while *she'd* been born a mere mortal.

She studied the ad again. She *wanted* to believe it, but did she dare trust its claims? *What if it's a trick? Can a flying-horse necklace really be the key to immortality?* Medusa wondered.

"Doubt it!" she muttered aloud.

A godboy sitting nearby overheard and gave her a sideways glance. She shot him a quick glare that made him widen his eyes and nervously look away.

It was Friday, last period, and the amphitheater was filled with immortal students—all of them beautiful, powerful, and awesome, with softly glittering skin. How she longed to be like them!

Sure, she went to MOA too. She was one of the few lucky mortals allowed to attend the Academy. Yet she had no true magical powers, like those of a goddess. Still, with a glance, she *could* turn a mortal to stone. That was something, at least. And she was the only student with snakes growing from the top of her head instead of hair! Glancing around, she idly reached up and twirled one of the snakes around her finger.

Usually school dramas were performed here in the amphitheater, but today the entire student body had gathered on the bleachers because of Career-ology Week. (Or *Job-ology* Week, as the students called it.) All week long, various speakers had come to MOA to talk about their jobs. Yesterday the god Hermes had spoken about his chariot delivery service.

Today the goddess Hera was here speaking about her wedding shop in the Immortal Marketplace. The regal-looking shop-goddess had thick blond hair styled high upon her head and a no-nonsense look in her eye. Although she wasn't unusually tall, something about her made her seem statuesque. Probably her confidence.

As Hera explained how she went about planning a wedding at Hera's Happy Endings, Medusa was only half listening. She shifted behind some other MOA students sitting in front of her so she was better hidden from Hera's view.

Sneakily, she reread the ad. It was maddeningly short on details about how the Immortalizer worked—if it worked at all. She'd almost be willing to risk disappointment if only it didn't cost so much. Thirty drachmas was a lot of money! Her weekly allowance was only three oboli—half a drachma. At the moment, she only had eight drachmas saved up.

"Any questions?" Hera asked the crowd.

Medusa jolted to attention and peered around the godboy in front of her. Seeing that the talk was nearly over, she set her scrollazine on the bench. Although the bleachers were packed with students, there was an empty space on either side of her. No one ever got too close to a girl with snake hair.